Frank Ronan

Frank Ronan was born in 1963 in Ireland. THE MEN WHO LOVED EVELYN COTTON, his first novel, won the 1989 *Irish Times*/Aer Lingus Literature Prize and is followed by A PICNIC IN EDEN, THE BETTER ANGEL, DIXIE CHICKEN and a collection of stories, HANDSOME MEN ARE SLIGHTLY SUNBURNT. He has had short stories published in a variety of magazines, in the collection TELLING STORIES 2, and broadcast on BBC Radio 4.

SCEPTRE

Also by Frank Ronan and published by Sceptre

A Picnic in Eden
The Better Angel
Dixie Chicken
Handsome Men Are Slightly Sunburnt

The Men Who Loved Evelyn Cotton

FRANK RONAN

SCEPTRE

British Library Cataloguing in Publication Data

Ronan, Frank
  Men Who Loved Evelyn Cotton – New ed
  I. Title
  823.914 [F]

ISBN 0 340 59909 X

Printed and bound in Great Britain by
Cox and Wyman Ltd, Reading, Berkshire

Hodder and Stoughton
A division of Hodder Headline PLC
338 Euston Road
London NW1 3BH

THE MEN WHO LOVED
EVELYN COTTON

I HAVE BEEN in love with Evelyn Cotton for twenty-four years and four months less eight days. We have made love twice. The first time was twenty-three years ago. The second time was yesterday. Does that make this a sad story: make me a comic figure?

I am constantly astonished that I have grown to be as old as I am. That I have avoided starvation; not only that, but lived to see my children launched on this world, witnessed the abdication of my hair, the formation of a middle-aged man who is set in his ways. I am a long way still from the menopause, if such a thing exists, but sometimes, in the bath, I stare down at myself, unable to believe that this is me, deteriorating, just as I stared at myself when I was thirteen, unable to believe that I was growing.

This is not a novel about the disillusion of middle age. This is not even a book about me. Where would I find enough in my life to fill two hundred pages? My life, so far, has been nothing. No, this is not self-pity or nihilism. It is just that my life has been in suspension for a long time. Survival, for me, has been a meaningless ritual.

I have spent my life in a waiting room; on a railway platform. I have gone through the motions of living like a man who is killing time until he can be somewhere else. I used to think that it was because I loved Evelyn Cotton. I thought she was the spinning-wheel that had pricked me and would be the prince who woke me. If the metaphor is transexual, then let it be. What did I care who penetrated whom, so long as some day we would be joined

1

gether. I have waited almost a quarter of a century. In that time, a man can be conceived and grow and begin to fade away again. If Evelyn had a daughter, I could be married to her by now. My sons are taller than I ever was. I am out of date. My built-in obsolescence has caught up with me.

If I seem a tedious man, or excessively depressed, I do not mean to be. It will pass. It is only because of yesterday. It seems reasonable to me now that yesterday would be the disaster it was. If you did something once when you were twenty, and if you realized at that moment that it was the happiest moment of your life, then that in itself is a crushing thought to have. You will never be happier. This is as good as it is going to get, if you are lucky. You wait twenty-three years to do it again. In the mean time you are married. You have children and you make money. For twenty-three years, each time you penetrate your wife you are trying to recall that once with Evelyn Cotton. Each of your children was conceived while you thought about Evelyn Cotton: abstract; detailed. There were times when you wept in the middle of fucking. It made Sally love you more because she thought that your tears were for her. You can't say that your tears are because of her; because of who she isn't. How can you tell someone who is fond of you that your life with them is only half a life?

And twenty-three years ago I had a tight, hard stomach and hair halfway down my forehead. Benedict Cotton was a wordless infant for whom we were hushed in our lovemaking. His cot was within a hand's reach of the bed that groaned beneath us. Our love was conducted in the faint smell of nappies, in my seething urgency, in her generous, unembarrassed pleasure. Yesterday, twenty-three years later, she was still the same. She had hardly changed. We were like Dorian Gray and his painting. I had changed for both of us. She was still as soft, as unhurried, as extraordinary. I was an old man full of nerves. Terrified by my dream come true.

Evelyn Cotton is my heroine. If you were living in this world, she might be yours. As it is, you have only read her books and seen her on your television. You, as the public, love her or hate her. She engenders strong emotion in other people. When you see her, you write to your Member of Parliament. When I see her, I tremble and have an erection. I know her well.

Perhaps I am the only one, apart from herself, who knows her at

2

all. I may have only been inside her twice, but I am the one she always came to for advice. Her only true friend. She spent her life giving advice to the rest of the world. Her books have changed millions of lives. Her thoughts and writings have the reputation of being seminal, which is not to say that they are original, but that they were expressed in a way which makes them easy to understand and tempting to put into practice. I have often seen my own thoughts, my own character in her writing, but she could put things in a way that I never could.

Is this to be the story of Evelyn's life? If it is, then I suppose that I am the person most qualified to write it. I was always everyone's confidant. I kept my own secrets to myself and allowed other people to do the talking. I have the reputation of being a shoulder you can cry on. This is simply because I was always afraid to bore anyone else with the details of my life. If you have nothing to tell, then you must listen. They all came to me in their troubles: Julius Drake in tears on my sofa; Hugh Longford in my kitchen with his charming condescension. He was the one who told me most in the end. He told me his dreams, his nightmares, his life, his future, his fear of himself. I know Hugh Longford as if I had written his character in a book. As if he had never existed and was invented by me. Benedict Cotton thinks of me as his favourite uncle. He is closer to me than my own sons are. This doesn't surprise me. My fondness for Benedict goes back to when I was wholly alive. My sons are part of this half life. I don't know if I actually believe that they exist.

Benedict is the image of his mother. If there are times when I feel more than just affection for him, then it is only because there are times when I almost feel that he and Evelyn are the same person. He has the same slow, contented way of looking at you. He is amused by the same combinations of words. The same smile transforms the same face.

I suppose that is us. We are the four men who have had substantial parts in Evelyn's life. If we all write books, then there will be four gospels. I won't be mentioned in any of the other three, until the very end. Although I know them better than anyone, Julius, Hugh and Benedict know nothing about me. It is as though I have always seen them through a two-way mirror. I am nothing to them.

3

There was a fifth man, but he is long gone from our lives. He was Benedict's father. He was my best friend, someone I grew up with who never grew up with me. It was through him that I met Evelyn in the first place. He was the catalyst who started us all off on this course. He set off this chain of events and then went away to enjoy himself elsewhere.

Ten thousand days ago seems as relevant a moment as any to go back to. In those days of heart-rending naïvety, we never imagined that we could be as we are now. My life was something that happened between 1960 and 1965. It was a student life of the clichéd sort, full of beer and innocence. Luck was a girl who would go the whole way with you and not get pregnant. There weren't many who achieved this. Simmy nearly did.

Simmy was handsome and working class. We all thought that it was a perfect combination of attributes. He was more articulate than the rest of us. When I think of him now, I can see that he had chips on his shoulders and that he was out to prove himself. At the time we all envied him. I don't know why he singled me out as a friend. Perhaps he thought that I was not such a snob as the rest. Perhaps it was genuine affection. It doesn't matter any more.

Simmy was a year or two older than me. He was a year or two more advanced in the dishonesty which we all learn in order to survive. We went to outlandish places together, like Greece and Turkey. We became quite inseparable at one point. That was just before our friendship was blown apart by the arrival of Benedict Cotton.

I had hardly noticed Evelyn at first. She was only another girlfriend of Simmy's. Girlfriends came and went, and there was no reason to think that Evelyn would be different. Simmy didn't even pretend to be infatuated with her.

Then there was one day when he came in to the Buttery with his face covered in a huge loose foolish grin. He sat down opposite me and gave me a friendly kick beneath the table. 'I've done it,' he said. I knew instantly what he meant. I asked him what it was like. I asked him with whom and when and where and how. He wasn't shy with details. There was nobody sitting near us and so he described the lot. The colour of her nipples. The way she had lain across the bed. The things she had cried out at the end. There was a struggle in me between envy and congratulation. He had barely

4

been going out with her for a week. He had succeeded in what was my wildest dream. I couldn't take my eyes off him, studying him to see if he was any different and trying to remember how he had been the day before. It had always been my assumption that manhood was something that was acquired in the first complete sexual encounter. According to my theory, the Simmy who now sat before me was a total man for the first time. I could see no difference, except that he was out of his head with happiness, and that he was slightly gloating about knowing something that I didn't.

I began to take notice of Evelyn Cotton. So much for love at first sight. I had her marked down as a girl who was willing to do it. I evolved a fantasy where she and Simmy had a terrible fight, and I moved in to pick up the pieces. I would put one arm around her shoulder and another up her dress.

It isn't until you begin to look at someone that you see them properly. Evelyn wasn't one of those girls who came into the room and everyone noticed. She was the sort whose looks improved with acquaintance. She became exquisite with familiarity. She had large faded grey eyes and thick auburn hair and heavy, dark skin. She barely spoke at all and, when she did, her voice was almost inaudibly soft. I was convinced that she would fall in love with me. But she never did.

None of it seemed to matter at the time. She was only one of a list of girls whom I hoped might one day seduce me and relieve me of my boyhood. I was not in love with her in the least but, because we were both so much in Simmy's company, we became good friends. This all lasted for a year or so. The three of us went to parties together and on expeditions. When Evelyn's parents came up to Oxford to see her, I had to pretend to be her boyfriend, because they would have disapproved so much of Simmy.

Her father was a retired army man, quite dotty with repression. Her mother was a bright, amusing snob. To us, in those days, they seemed perfectly ordinary. That was what parents were supposed to be like, but preferably with more money. Mine were exactly the same. Perhaps that is why Evelyn never loved me. I was too close to her own suffocating background. I was the sort of person she was trying to escape from. Simmy seemed an ideal escape route. He spoke with an unashamed Yorkshire voice and held his knife like a pencil, unabashed. He could scratch his balls in mixed company and seem no less charming for it. Our admiration for him was boundless. He seemed to be the king of St Catherine's and the remedy for those dinosaurs at Teddy Hall. He seemed to embody a freedom that could never be achieved by the upper classes. People like Evelyn and me had always been taught to emulate the aristocracy. Our rebellion was to emulate Simmy.

By and by I met a girl named Sally who was at the same secretarial college as Evelyn. Sally was an obliging sort of girl and it wasn't long until I had crossed my phantom threshold into manhood. There was no clap of thunder, but I did feel that my life had a sort of completeness (although I could see no difference in the mirror). For a moment there was something like perfection. If only we could have all gone on like that. If we could have held our personal lives at that level.

If ifs and ands.

BENEDICT COTTON WAS conceived in a tree. It was a common oak, known in Latin as *Quercus robur*. I had done my best to prevent it happening. I had an instinct that something was going to destroy all our happiness. Simmy had been staying with me, at the house of my parents. He was restless and discontented. There had been a terrible fight with Evelyn.

I can see it all. It was Saturday and Somerset. We were out for a walk along the lanes. The main road was two fields away. Simmy announced suddenly that he was going to see Evelyn. She lived about twenty miles away, down the A303. She was home that weekend. Simmy leaped over a gate and began to walk towards the main road to begin hitch-hiking.

I called to him. I said don't go. I pleaded with him and called him a bastard. I tried everything I could to make him stay with me. Perhaps it was just because I was beginning to resent the power that Evelyn had over him. She wasn't just a girlfriend to him any more. He was beginning to enjoy her company. I suspected that he preferred her company to mine. What could I do for him compared with her? I was only a friend. She was a friend and bedmate and bottlewasher. She would type up his notes for him and play footsie at the same time. There was nothing I could do but drink beer and talk politics. I had no way of persuading him not to go and see Evelyn.

It wasn't until months later that Simmy reminded me of this scene. I had forgotten it in the mean time. He said, 'Guess what? Evelyn is pregnant.'

He had an expression of matter-of-fact pride on his face. He was torn between fear and boastfulness. I was torn between congratulation and commiseration. I said, 'I hope Evelyn isn't being difficult about it.'

He told me that Evelyn was being extremely difficult. She had shouted at him twice. She had threatened to telephone his parents. As usual, he gave me all the details. He claimed the conception had happened the day that I had tried to prevent him from seeing her. This pleased me enormously. He could see that I had his best interests at heart, even on a telepathic level. We conspired to escape from Evelyn before she could trap him. It was all quite old-fashioned and touching. Friends sticking by each other through thick and thin. We laughed at the idea of conception in a tree. We decided to run away together in search of adventure and less troublesome women.

You see, in a way, I had betrayed Evelyn before I had even begun. I have always had the guilt of starting out on the wrong side. But I was terribly young. Almost a child. I knew that women were not to be trusted. Their only ambition was to trap themselves a husband. And this was true of most of the girls at smart secretarial colleges in Oxford in those days. I thought that, by allowing herself to become pregnant, Evelyn was risking more in her bid to be married than most girls would dare. I thought that it was only right she should be thwarted and punished. Poor Simmy. It wasn't him who was pregnant, why should he have been the one to suffer?

It was the end of term. Simmy and I set off on a spree through France. I forgot about Evelyn. Simmy seemed to have forgotten her as well, except that our tent was often filled with his roaring nightmares, and he became more and more disconnected from me, until we could hardly speak at all. And something else happened that summer. It was perhaps a symptom of the way in which we were drifting apart, but in any case it sealed the gulf between us. I am not sure of the details. We were drunk at the time, but that is not the only reason I have forgotten it. I locked it away in my mind and never thought of it until now, and now it is black with darkness and my own inhibition. What can I tell you about this sparse, dusty memory?

I don't think that anything really happened. It was more to do with an awareness that something might happen. Perhaps Simmy was trying to escape from the disaster of his heterosexuality in the oak tree. Perhaps he was trying to shed his guilt in some way. Perhaps in his drunken sleep he thought that I was someone else. But I had no way of analysing it at the time. I was frightened and horrified. The event is all confusion in my mind. Memory is unreliable when it comes this close to the bone. I remember a night of me striding around a Dordogne field, pretending to be angry to hide my sadness and fear.

Perhaps it was all for the best. I saw that women were not the only people capable of betrayal. The human race was levelled out and my mind was free of the idea that men were in some way morally superior, or that friendship was a purer, finer thing than sex. Perhaps that was the time when I began to see Evelyn's side of things, and to know what it was like to be at the sharp, helpless end of the instrument.

There was no way of continuing the holiday after this. We made a gruff, masculine peace in the morning; we tried to laugh about it and called it a drunken misunderstanding. We kept up pretences for a day or two, and it seemed fine in the daytime, but the lack of sleep was telling on me, and I made an excuse for going back to England early that was so puerile I have forgotten it. I think that Simmy was relieved to see me go. I had become as silent as him. I have met him only once since that time, and I found that he had become hollow and alien to me. The spark that all of us had found so attractive at Oxford was gone from him.

Sally was seeing another man when I got back. He was an effete highbrow from Balliol. She was swanking about in the best circles. It didn't matter to me, or affect my happiness. When you are young, misery is a pleasure in itself. Rejection was something to be wallowing in; depression was an interesting state of mind. I wrote a lot of poetry and stuff in my final year, and none of it pertained to Sally. She was no heap of wheat set about with lilies. She was no loss to me. The young are very cold and careless.

Sometimes I wondered what had become of Evelyn. I did not imagine that I would ever see her again. Even so, I was now on her side, if there were sides to be taken. I dreamt about her once or twice. You don't dream about people unless they are significant to you.

Sally was dumped by her highbrow in December, and I began to see her again. That is the way it has been with Sally and me. We have constantly drifted into each other's lives. We eventually got married because it seemed to be our fate. If I went to live in a certain part of London, Sally would be there before me, by coincidence. Marrying her was like accepting the inevitable. But none of that was to happen for a while yet. In December, Sally told me where Evelyn had gone to have her baby. That was the moment when love reared its ugly head. How else can I explain my reaction? I had an overwhelming compulsion to go and see her. It was curiosity and guilt and charity and old affection. I had such a mixture of good and bad motives that I didn't actually want to go. But I was compelled to go. I had fallen in love.

Drag yourself back to the early Sixties, if you are old enough to remember them. I can't help thinking that the world must be a better place now, in these days when a child is someone in his own right and doesn't need his father's surname to make him respectable. Evelyn and Benedict Cotton were inmates of an institute in Clapham run by the Church of England for naughty girls. When I went to see her, Benedict was two weeks old. She had been in the home for eight weeks. I was her first visitor.

She was surprised to see me. Thrilled. I have never seen a face light up like that at my arrival anywhere. I had to wait downstairs while the matron fetched her. We went walking on Clapham Common. I don't know what it was. I suddenly felt important in her life. I could do things for her. There is nothing in this life like the first day you are in love. It can only happen once. If it has happened to you, then you know how I felt. If you have never had the experience, then it is no use my explaining it to you. It is pure slush. Wait and see.

Normally, visitors weren't allowed into the nursery to see the babies, but when we got back to the home the matron had gone out, and Evelyn brought Benedict down for me to see. Babies. The way I reacted to Benedict you would have thought he was my own. The other girls there assumed that I was the father. I was too pleased with myself to disabuse them.

Then Evelyn explained that the purpose of the whole exercise was adoption. What could I say? It wasn't my place to persuade her to keep Benedict. Who was I to foist an infant on a single girl? I felt

10

a thread of hatred for Simmy. I stammered. Embarrassment showed instead of the anger I felt. I left that place and Evelyn and Benedict, shaking with my own impotence.

I have never had such a journey as on that train back to Oxford. I almost had a brainstorm. I was furious with Simmy. I wanted to kill Evelyn's parents. They were just letting her get on with it until she could return to them with her respectability regained. Nothing more would ever be said about the unfortunate episode, and they would try their best to find her a nice husband. I wanted to plant a bomb in the maternity wing of Tooting Bec Hospital, where the sister had called Evelyn a whore. I decided to punch the nose of the next Trinity man to refer to girls as fruit.

This was all blather. It wasn't my conversion to feminism or anything like it. What I really wanted to do was marry Evelyn and adopt Benedict and Get Rich Quick to support them. I even considered a career in advertising, would you believe. I could see us all with roses round the door and Benedict on the floor. By Oxford, my head was swimming with resolution.

But I was beaten to her. While I was planning our lives, Evelyn was actually doing something about it. She married a don.

This husband of Evelyn's came out of nowhere. I have never met him, but she told me about him afterwards. There have been few marriages as short or as unsatisfactory; though in a way, they both got what they wanted out of it, for a while.

He was produced by an old flatmate of Evelyn's. They turned up in Clapham the day after I had. He was a man of about fifty, stooped and a little disconnected. He was kind to Evelyn and deferential. He returned on his own the next day and proposed to her.

Why she couldn't have waited for me? Why I didn't come to her rescue, or even write or telephone sooner? It was nearly Christmas and nearly the time to give Benedict away to strangers. She grasped at this man's straw and left Clapham to become his ready-made family.

Evelyn Cotton began and ended her married life in a large old house in Oxford where she saw her husband from time to time, mostly in the distance. He barely spoke to her, and she and Benedict were given a room together at the top of the house far from his own bedroom. An envelope would be lying on the hall

11

table every Tuesday with the week's housekeeping money inside. There was no one to feed but herself. The don never ate at home. He looked as though he hardly ate at all. A taciturn middle-aged woman came to do the housework. There was nothing for Evelyn to do but look after Benedict.

The don had a fixation about keeping his clothes clean. When he was at home he spent a lot of his time in his room changing into clean shirts and socks and underwear and scrubbing the garments he had just removed in the washbasin. There were nearly always clothes drying in front of his electric fire and the ironing board was taken out for each article as it dried, and then folded back again. The don allowed no one but himself to touch his clothes. His greatest pleasure was to have every piece of cloth in his possession laundered and neatly folded in their drawers. To achieve this he had to work late into the night, stark naked. On the mornings following these orgies he would often be late for a lecture, because he was so reluctant to soil the perfection of his wardrobe by wearing any of its contents.

From the moment she set foot in his house, he barely noticed Evelyn. He would look cross sometimes if Benedict was crying, but would say nothing.

If I tell you that Evelyn Cotton was relieved and grateful you might find that difficult to believe. This woman who is now the champion of feminist thought around the world. But even she was nineteen years old once. She had been an unmarried mother in a society that still clung to Victorian values. Even if it hadn't been for her mistake, a comfortable marriage would have been the best she could have hoped for. She was relieved at being able to keep her son. She was relieved not to have to work as a secretary. She was relieved not to be a withering spinster. Someone else was taking care of her life and her future and her expenses and the house she lived in. She had relief up to her eyeballs, and she couldn't see beyond it.

For a while she thought that she had made it. She borrowed twelve pounds from the bank and bought herself a Mary Quant suit. There was always plenty left over from the housekeeping to have her hair constructed every week. Once or twice it occurred to her to wonder who she was doing it all for. But she was too relieved at the security of her position to allow any incisive analysis

of her circumstances. Her fingernails had never been so beautif[ully]
tended. A baby was never so much in its mother's company. Time
had never been so cheap and plentiful.

There was an odd flurry of intelligence in her mind when she
would be sitting at the front window of the house and a girl of her
own age would walk past, wearing the same large jersey and ski
pants that she herself had worn and still wore, but also that air of
being single, of being another species. Some small feeling of
having lost as well as gained crept into her mind. Some fear that
her life was not only taken care of: that it might be ended. She
wondered if she had drawn her lot and if this was all she would
ever have. It got no better.

But it could have been worse. Evelyn Cotton was grateful for
what she had. As a writer, she evolved a theory of life in which
gratitude was the greatest single evil. Gratitude which is imposed
on women to keep them in their place. I shouldn't need to explain
this to you. Read any one of her books and you will find that she
explains it much better than I ever could.

It could have been boredom that drove her away from the don. It
could have been that she realised the preposterousness of her
position. She had assumed at first that he had married her for sex,
and she waited week after week for him to demand his conjugal
right. When it became plain that he had no interest in her body, or
in her ability as a housekeeper, or her companionship, she began
to be uneasy. She had no obvious function, and seemed to be
giving him nothing in return for his patronage. She wondered if he
was dissatisfied with her in some way, but was too polite to say so.
She felt at times as though she had defrauded him, at times as
though he had defrauded her.

I wish that I had come across her at this time. I was still at
Oxford. I can't have been far away. But the don never brought her
out, and never brought his friends home, if he had any. Most of the
people we had known the year before had moved on or gone down.
It may have been loneliness that drove her away from the don.

Sometimes, in desperation, she talked to the woman next door.
This sharp, nosy old woman had the disturbing habit of opening
their conversations by asking, 'Happy, are you?' in a knowing voice
that you knew would one day say I told you so. And then one day
the woman told her so.

13

out of the house that day to find her neighbour
down-at-heel girl holding a small child by the hand.
peared, the girl fled.

are you?' said the neighbour. 'That was your pre-
hat was. She stayed a long time, that one. They don't
usually ay as long as she did.'

And it all came out. She discovered her function in the don's
life. She was thrown out of her complacency and gratitude. She
was only the latest in a long line of single mothers whom he had
married to complete his idea of a household. She was part of his
delusion of order, as much as the shelves of ironed shirts and
collars. She could be replaced the next day by any girl with any
child and the don would see no difference.

She was silent for a day or two. She thought that she only
needed to adjust herself to her role, now that she knew what it was.
It was up to her to make the best of things. There were people in
worse circumstances than she. Her life was not impossible.
Perhaps she could find a friend or take a lover.

But she must, in some subconscious department of her mind,
have wanted to escape. She decided to go home to Somerset for a
day or two. Her reason was that she hadn't seen her parents in
eight months. That they had never seen Benedict, or congratulated
her on her marriage.

She went to the don, and told him that she was going to visit her
parents. It was like being at school and asking permission to go to
the lavatory. He sighed, and said if she must she must, as though
he didn't believe her but couldn't be responsible for her wetting
her knickers all the same. He gave her money for the train.

When she went to say goodbye to him, he was standing naked at
his armoires, counting up his handkerchiefs. Because of her
extreme short-sightedness she didn't notice his nudity until she
was up close to him, and then it was too late to do anything but
feign normality. Her last impression of him was a flaccid, raw and
creased body, and a face that accused her of betrayal.

CONSIDERING HOW DEEPLY ashamed they were to see her, Evelyn's parents made a commendably brave show of her visit. Her mother was constantly trying to think of nice things to say about the baby, and her father was kind enough to say nothing at all. Benedict was a large, healthy baby, all fat and smiles. There was no pretending that he might be newborn and, even if he was, the whole village had seen her as a single girl eight months before.

They didn't specifically say that Evelyn wasn't to take her baby out for walks, but they somehow made it a lot easier if Evelyn went for walks on her own. People who had been due to visit them were put off. They had to cancel a dinner party. But they tried to bear it all cheerfully, and not ask Evelyn too often when she was going back to Oxford.

They had their answer on the third day of her visit. A van arrived in the village, containing all of Evelyn's belongings. Still, they tried to be nice about it and not ask any questions. And if her mother said that she had suspected something like this was afoot, she said it in an unguarded moment.

Evelyn was as surprised as anyone to have her things returned to her. The letter from the don's solicitor which talked about divorce shocked her deeply. And then again she was relieved. Not having to go back to Oxford was a great release to her. The pressure of being with her parents was almost bearable because of the novelty of it. But, on the other hand, she was trying their bravery to the limit. They went about with white knuckles, whispering to each other.

Evelyn began to dream that Benedict had been killed. Her parents wouldn't tell her what they had done with the body, but kept reassuring her that it was all for the best. These dreams seemed disturbingly likely to her, and she began to look about her for the next frying pan within leaping distance.

She met Charles Felix as they were both avoiding church in the same rustic laneway. I think they had known each other vaguely as children. Their parents all lived in the same village.

Perhaps Charles Felix was fond of Evelyn. He stepped into her life at just the moment when she most needed an heroic rescue. He gathered her and Benedict up and whisked them off to Bristol within days of their meeting. It sounds like love at first sight. But have we decided yet if we believe in the existence of love?

One of the reasons I had almost broken my heart over Evelyn when she was in Clapham was that I thought she was a spoiled creature in the eyes of the world. I thought that no man would want to marry her. I thought that no man would rear another man's child. I was prepared to make a great sacrifice of my own respectability, out of my love and pity for Evelyn. I was surprised, then, to find that she was in demand. Men seemed to be drawn to this unmarried mother in droves. It seems that if you are a girl and want a husband, and any old husband will do, you must first have a child. Perhaps it is because your fertility is proven. Perhaps a man will feel that he has the upper hand from the beginning. Perhaps these men require gratitude above everything in their partner. And, also, it is nice to feel that you are doing someone a favour.

I don't mean to be nasty about Charles Felix. He may not have given Evelyn security, but he did give her a feeling of normality. She was allowed to do his laundry for him. In that sense he was an improvement on the don. But, on the other hand, he became involved with Evelyn within days of his old girlfriend moving out on him. Evelyn was a convenient replacement. Perhaps there was no love in this arrangement.

Charles Felix was a painter. He had a large studio in Clifton near the suspension bridge, and lived there in romantic rather than abject poverty. By curious coincidence I had gone to school with him once. He was charming, I suppose. He knew how to deal with people like Evelyn's parents and his own. He gave the impression when he was in Somerset that he kept a large establishment in

Clifton, and that he wanted to engage Evelyn as his housekeeper. I doubt if Evelyn's parents believed him. They knew the genteel poverty of the Felixes which was the same as their own. And Charles Felix was one of the first people to have long hair, which made it seem unlikely that he kept any kind of establishment at all.

But they were relieved to have the worry and embarrassment of Evelyn living at home taken off their hands. It was considered the best thing all round, and so they condemned their daughter to be an artist's skivvy and consort, and then they went back to thinking about bridge and alstroemerias.

Evelyn did not have a propitious beginning to her domestic reign in Clifton. When she and Benedict entered the studio for the first time, the floor was littered with Felix's trousers and underclothes, all with the crotches neatly snipped out of them. There was an obscene remark written across the big window in lipstick, inverted to be read from the outside. The china was smashed. It seemed that Charles's previous girlfriend had been cross about being forced to leave.

Felix was so shocked by the state of his flat that he was forced to got out for a drink there and then. Evelyn kindly said that she would see what she could do to clear it up by the time he came back. Perhaps that was why he stayed out so long, to give her time to clear up properly. He arrived back in the early hours to find her patiently stitching together what she could of his trousers. He complimented her by telling her that she was a good girl. He could see they were going to get on.

I don't think that Felix was a bad sort. He liked to have a girl around the place like anyone else. For all his bohemian appearance he was fond of cooked breakfasts and clean linen. He gave Evelyn a function in life. She got a nice job, typing for an estate agent, which kept them in food and rent. Occasionally, Felix would get some money from his parents, and then he would rush home to her with champagne in one arm and a lemon tree in the other. He knew how to make a girl happy.

I met Evelyn by chance soon after she had moved to Clifton. I had given up hope of ever seeing her again, and there she was, in Milsom Street, Bath, with Felix beside her. I ran towards them. I blathered and flustered at them and made no sense. They stood in front of me, watching as though I were a bizarre street act, failing to entertain them.

Benedict was a fat baby in a pram. Felix was carrying an enormous bundle of daffodils. Evelyn peered at me. Her sight was so bad that she was unable to make out who I was. It was Felix who recognised me first. He remembered me winning the poetry prize at school. Then I recognised him and remembered him for being expelled. He had hung the matron's daughter out of a second-floor window while she had been divested of her upper clothing, on Parents' Day.

It was while we were reminiscing about our schooldays that Evelyn began to realise who I was.

For months and months, I had wished for nothing more than to see her again. I had long speeches and short, heart-rending phrases composed and memorised in anticipation of this moment. But now that I had met her, nothing was right. I was faced with Charles Felix's drawling confidence. He was seven inches taller than me. He was plainly better looking than me; more dashing; he had a deep, lazy voice. He seemed to have a control of his life that was remarkable for a person of his age. I felt as though I was squeaking and jumping up and down on the pavement like a frog. I had rushed up to them because I had wanted Evelyn and Benedict to come away with me. But for what? I was still a student. I had nothing to give them. And Felix was stroking her hair in an absent-minded, possessive way, and smiling at me as though he was proud of his possession. She looked as though she was perfectly happy where she was. What could I say? Whenever I did say anything, Felix would laugh. I didn't know at the time whether he found me amusing or laughable.

I became great friends with Evelyn and Charles. I managed to get a job in Bath for the summer, and I sublet a tiny room from them to live in. It wasn't the most convenient place for me to stay. It was completely overcrowded with the four of us and I had to do a lot of commuting. But I was near Evelyn and I could have asked for nothing else. Well, perhaps one other thing.

This was a time of the most exquisite happiness and the most unbearable frustration for me. I had hours on end alone with Evelyn, of talking and soul-searching and all that stuff that is so riveting to the young. I began to realise how intelligent she was.

18

That she was a lot cleverer than me or Charles, but her cleverness was latent and disguised, as though she herself was frightened by it. She was filling the role she had been given with a mania for perfection. The studio began to look more like an illustration from *House & Garden* than a bohemian den. Things were washed and scrubbed as soon as they had been used. She sat up until late at night making clothes for Benedict and herself. I still have the jersey that she knitted for me that summer.

I meant no more to her than I had meant when she was going out with Simmy. Except that I had not been in love with her in those days. Now, in Clifton, I never knew whether I was happy or not, but at least I was certain that I was fully alive. My senses and emotions were constantly scraped raw. The middles of my nights were barbed with the sound of Evelyn's lovemaking. The soft heavy groaning and the occasional coloratura soprano. In the mornings I had to pass them in their bed to get to the bathroom. He, snoring with an arm thrown behind his head, and an arm thrown carelessly across her. She, blinking out into the world from beneath the tortured mass of her hair, a white globe of breast appearing among the sheets for a tantalising moment, a foot withdrawn to cover. Me, wandering through as casually as I could, holding my towel in front of the morning stiffness, bidding a cheerful good morning and only just preventing myself from doing something stupid.

I thought that if I was there, and if I saw her every day, she would surely love me. First she would know me, and then she would love me. I remained month after month in Clifton, and I was nearly insane. She might at least have taken me on as an occasional lover, if only to revenge herself on Felix.

We often sat up entire nights, Evelyn and I, waiting for him together. She thought that he was only out drinking, but I knew exactly what he was up to. He was always boasting to me of his conquests. I sat with her, on the chair opposite, longing to make a move, but terrified of destroying everything. Once, I told her about how I had planned to rescue her and Benedict from the home in Clapham. Marry her, and support them both.

She told me that I was awfully sweet.

I felt as though I was six years old and had presented her with something for the nature table. I wanted to leap off my chair and expose myself to her; ravage her and force her to see me as I was.

But I sat, and said politely would she like more coffee. At five or six in the morning we would hear him stumbling on the stairs and the click of the lower door, and I would slide away to bed and leave her to face him alone. A short while later I would hear the rhythm of her voice as he rammed his apology home.

I was a wreck by September. I had lost nearly three stones and my hair was coming out in handfuls. I decided to move to London and get a better job and have a life of my own. The day that I left, I declared my love to her and begged her to come with me. I stood weeping on her threshold.

She told me that I was awfully sweet.

THE NEXT TIME I saw her she was a different person. Something had clicked over inside of her and it was plain that she had had enough of that whole system of life. She was smoking heavily and the flat was a mess. I think she may have been taking drugs of some kind, although she always denies this.

I had called in at the flat on the off-chance. She and Benedict were alone. Felix had gone down to his parents' for the weekend. I had called because I was almost ready to kill myself. In the months since I had seen her my obsession with her had grown daily. I had hoped to forget her, but every night I had a dream of her. My dream was usually of a sexual disaster, followed by her anger.

For the second time, she was delighted to see me. She answered the door wearing only a man's shirt. She looked extraordinary in it. I think those were the days just before the mini skirt. Certainly, I had never seen anything like it before. That afternoon is imprinted in me: she, crosslegged and barelegged on the bed, sucking at cigarettes and talking to me as though I was human. It was the clearest brightest spring day. We were surrounded by yellow Felix paintings and Benedict threw brushes across the floor and chortled. I sat, strained to the end of my elasticity and trying to seem normal. We talked and drank terrible coffee. I don't think that I really heard a word she said, I was so pulverised by her presence.

Evening came. I had brought wine, which we drank, but not

21

much. The effort of being near her was exhausting me. I was either trying to tear my eyes away from her in case I was leering, or trying to prop them open in case I dropped off to sleep. She asked me if I wanted to stay in the flat.

I said if it wasn't any trouble.

She said it was no trouble. I would have to sleep on the floor. My old room was full of junk.

I said that anything was fine. And then she kissed me.

I suppose everyone has been in heaven once in their life. It is a terrible thing to look down from that height of ecstasy and know that it doesn't matter if you die now because you will never be happier. In amongst the crushing ecstasy is a rotten feeling that you are in possession of the only thing you have ever wanted. For the rest of your life, you are without a plan or ambition. From the moment she first kisses you, it is downhill all the way.

You used to spend a fortune on haircuts and neckties; spend hours perfecting a shaving technique. You remember the agony of a hundred daily sit-ups with your feet hooked beneath the end of the bed. You wanted to be such an extraordinary Adonis that sooner or later Evelyn would fall in love with you simply on account of your perfection. You knew that, sooner or later, she would have to see how appalling Felix was, with his paint-spattered baggy trousers and the small groves of unattended stubble on his great square chin and the strong smell of himself that he carried about with him.

Now, her arms and legs are wrapped around you. Her belly slides softly across yours, trapping small bubbles of air between them. Her chin is dug into your clavicle. The rhythms of her voice that used to haunt you every night are rushing past your ear in gusts of warm breath. You think that, now that she knows what you can do for her, she will always be with you. How can she fail to love you once you have shot your most private essence inside of her? Isn't this what Cupid's arrow is in metaphor?

You have no idea that Evelyn Cotton is pregnant again. That she has no reason for sleeping with you except to revenge herself on Charles Felix who is insisting that she has an abortion. That it could have been you or it could have been anyone else. You are still too young and too much of a man to realise that there is nothing special about what you can do in bed. Like most men, you think that there is no one else like you. You still have romantic ideas about love and potency.

It is not your fault. All that steaming and groaning is very persuasive. Very misleading. In the morning when you lie in the damp heat of the bed, soaked in the smells you have created, and watch her washing herself at the basin: one hand to hold her skirt up and one hand to scrub – and that wet hollow noise – and her knees bent outwards and her hair falling over her face as she concentrates; when you watch her do this, you feel that she is yours. That she and Benedict will come away with you today.

It is as though you are wearing a laurel wreath. The sun is crowning you by beating strongly across the bed. You throw the blankets off to feel the heat of it on your skin. Your organ is tender and swollen with overuse, but you are as proud as if it was a battle scar. A spoil of triumph. Loot of conquest. You want her to turn around and see you naked because your body is her property now. Hers to admire. It is time to reap the fruit of all those millions of sit-ups which you have done for her sake.

She looked over towards me, asking if I was awake yet and, as she looked, she squinted to see if I was there at all. In puffing myself out I had forgotten her short-sightedness. She asked me if I was dressed yet.

What could I do in my disappointment, but unflex my stomach and put it all away? Benedict's waking scream dissolved the last shred of delusion in me. I was edging back towards my proper place. I said, out of desperation, 'Evelyn, will you come away with me?'

She said that she was sorry.

I said, 'Why not?'

'I don't love you,' she said.

As she said it, I knew that it was hollow. It may have been true that she didn't love me, but that wasn't the reason she wouldn't come away. I couldn't believe that she loved Charles Felix. If she did, why would she have slept with me?

'You don't love Charles either,' I said.

She said that she had to think of Benedict.

I suddenly realised that I was wrong. That if I wanted Evelyn to marry me I was never going to do it with haircuts and stomach muscles. It wasn't enough that I was going to be desperate about her and nice to her and be at home with her rather than out drinking with the men. I was earning a pittance. I lived in a black hole of a bedsit in Spitalfields. I was no good to her. She would have no business falling in love with me.

'I will make money,' I said.

'How?' she said, and I could see that she wasn't asking me how I could, but telling me that I couldn't. I had the feeling that I was too late.

I packed myself away into my clothes, feeling like a failed Hoover salesman packing his demonstration model back into the suitcase. I am sorry for taking up so much of your time, madam, but if you have a change of mind, here is my card.

For the second time, I left her with tears in my eyes and she told me I was awfully sweet, and I teetered on the railway platform at Temple Meads, wondering if it was time to step in front of the express and put an end to it, stomach muscles and all.

Do I seem obsessed with stomach muscles? Well, you should see me now. I have never come to terms with this hard, hairy sphere which I carry around in front of me. I don't know why it is there, or how to make it go away. I have sat in Turkish baths, surrounded by people who look like me, and I have sat on nautilus machines, surrounded by people who don't. I have eaten raw carrots until my skin turned orange, but I still carry this monstrous carbuncle like an inverted hunchback. I am convinced that it is not my stomach at all, but a giant tumour which God has sent to try me. Someday, if I am good, he will remove it.

THAT WAS THE day, in the spring of 1965, that I died. If I had jumped beneath a train at Temple Meads that day it would have made no difference. I sometimes feel guilty about all the space I have taken up and all the food I have spuriously eaten in this world. For twenty-three years it has been wasted on me. This self-pitying drivel can't interest you. From now on, I am out of the picture. I am only their confessional box, as dark and anonymous and forgiving. Over the years, whenever I phoned Evelyn (how odd – I have just realised that in twenty-three years she has never phoned me), she would talk to me for hours, telling me every detail of her life and every twinge of her conscience while she had me transfixed on the other end. It was masturbation and self-flagellation; balm and punishment. It was like a life-support machine that just barely, barely kept the spark of life in me going. And at the same time it suppressed that spark of life to an infinitesimal minuteness, so that I was still technically dead. But still, I am the most complete file there is on Evelyn Cotton's life. If we lived in a more scientifically advanced age, the University of Texas would buy my brain and keep it in their library, along with her manuscripts and letters. They could keep it in a designer brainbox, with a picture of me, aged twenty-one, on the front. More attractive than this rheumy-eyed forty-four year old. I have thick hair on my back and my toes have turned yellow. Enough of this decaying corpse in whom I am.

In chronological order, Julius Drake was the next man to come into Evelyn's life. He was an accountant who specialised in artists, and that was how she met him. Charles Felix was one of his clients.

In fact, Evelyn never did have that abortion. She miscarried just before she was due to have it. But the episode had opened her eyes to an ugly side in Felix, and made her feel the insecurity of her tenure. And, I suppose, she was bored. She didn't have an amazing life – typing all day, and housework every other waking hour, and miracles of loaves and fishes to keep the artist's strength up. The novelty of being made to stand by the window with no clothes on while someone made endless sketches of her had worn off. Especially as these sketches would be translated into yellow abstracts, titled 'Evelyn Nude', so that even though no one could see whether or not it was her, she still had the embarrassment of them knowing it was her.

She began to have an affair with Julius. At first it was only out of boredom and revenge. I find it difficult to explain what she saw in Julius Drake. Benedict told me recently that it was sex; that she only ran off with him for sex. I was so hurt by this interpretation of events that for a while I believed it. But, really, sex could have had little to do with it. When she did run away with Julius she was looking for a better life for herself and for Benedict. Perhaps she had been conned by Julius, or perhaps she was desperate. Let me tell you about Julius Drake.

Julius Drake was born in Hampstead of intellectual immigrant parents. I won't start a nature versus nurture argument here, but I do believe that a villain is born a villain, irredeemably, though I will grant you that there may be factors which will nudge his villainy in a certain direction.

He spent his youth wanting to write prose and win the Nobel prize and satisfy the intellectual snobbery of his parents. Because their friends were all of the genius class, they constantly made him feel inadequate, and were always pointing out to him, no matter how well he did, that he was not as clever as some. They gave him too much education and too many aesthetic preconceptions and expectations. They fossicked about in him too much for latent genius. He grew up to feel that he had no mental cavity which had not been scoured and filled.

His only real aptitude was for figures and his only deep interest the acquisition of wealth and its maintenance. His literary ambitions were something that had been imposed upon him by his parents.

On the face of it, he openly rebelled against his background and showed his independence of mind by becoming an accountant. In secret, he nourished his literary ambition and knew that one day he would show them. Someday, the things he would write and the books that were bound to be inside him would be the subject of whole courses at major universities. Acolytes and biographers would camp in his garden.

He could have gone halfway towards pleasing his parents. He could have become an architect, but he knew that they would only treat such a compromise with the derision it deserved. The only thing that would impress them would be the Swedish accolade. They would find it a nice surprise.

His idea, I will grant you, was a brilliant one. There were hundreds of scatterbrained and starving but marketable geniuses in England at the time. They were all producing work which, if it wasn't valuable at that moment, would become valuable in the future. None of them knew how to fill out a tax return, or had the money to pay an accountant. Julius knew these people through his parents. A lot of them were children he had grown up with.

The word got around that that nice Julius Drake (a little peculiar and boring – but he was an accountant) would sort out your finances and, in return, all he would ask for was a piece of your work. A painting or a rug or a bronze or, if you were a writer, a piece of copyright. He became an important background figure in the arts. Ask any painter or writer or carpet-maker from the Sixties and Seventies who was fashionable or promising at the time; who had credibility but no money in the bank. Ask them who their accountant was, and they will probably tell you (as a look of black irritation crosses their features) that it was Julius Drake. Some people still wonder whether he was a prop or a leech. I will be generous and say that they were jolly grateful for him at the time, and, if he abused their trust in later years, he made their lives a lot easier at the beginning. This may be the last time I will be generous about Julius. It is not my habit to speak well of him. I am perfectly nice to him, and he thinks of me as his best friend and closest confidant, but the fact is that I have hated him from the first

27

moment I saw him. I often think of tying him down and drawing his brains out through his nostrils with a wire hook.

Don't think that this means I am going to be prejudiced against him in what I tell you. I am perfectly capable of seeing things dispassionately and telling it as it was. Did I make Charles Felix sound any worse than was necessary? The fact is that Julius Drake is a ghastly man. Not only despicable, but pathetic with it. Take it from me. Or ask anyone.

When Evelyn first met him, his business was just gathering steam. The first of his clients had just become successful, and many others were about to. He forgave them all for their eventual success because it seemed to him that he had had a hand in it. He saw their success as stemming from his creativity and, in a way, as a guarantee of the success of his own art, once he'd got round to writing it. He also forgave the success of his clients because it made the pieces in his possession extraordinarily valuable. He never forgave Evelyn her success because it was nothing to do with him.

We are getting ahead of ourselves. Evelyn Cotton is still a short-sighted artist's floozie, who has just been spotted by Julius Drake. He was impressed by her. I suppose he may even have seen her as a sound investment. He could see that she was a wonderful mother to Benedict. She cooked the most fabulous meals out of scraps. She supported the household by typing. Felix, with his usual indiscretion, had boasted to Julius how steamy she was in bed. (When Julius told me this, it set me wondering about Felix. He only ever seemed to be sexually active when there were other people around. He would be content to paint landscapes for weeks on end but, as soon as I showed up, he would insist that Evelyn remove her clothes and model for him. I can't tell you what a dreadful effect that had on me. He was always boasting, somehow. Always leaving the bathroom door open and making the bed creak. I didn't find it odd at the time, because I was too besotted with Evelyn, but it seems distinctly odd to me now.) Julius set his cap at Evelyn. She was exactly the sort of person he was looking for.

Julius Drake was a single parent. Little Hannah Drake had killed her mother in labour. Julius's parents helped him to look after the child, but they were becoming old and doddery and in need of looking after themselves. At the moment they were paying for the services of a nanny for Hannah. Have I told you that they were rich? They were rolling in it; well, comfortable. Julius couldn't bear to see money being thrown away on wages (it affected his inheritance, after all), and so that was one problem that Evelyn could solve. Another thing that worried him was the amount of money he was spending on prostitutes. A chap can't help his libido, and Julius was a restless, energetic sort of character. He also worried about social diseases, but the money bothered him more. And then he thought that he could improve Evelyn's circumstances. That he would be doing her a favour.

This last point is important. Ghastly as Julius was, there was always a good intention lurking somewhere in his reasoning. Many people excuse him for this, but I can't. The biggest messes he made of other people's lives were because of this fatal combination of good intentions and strangling selfishness. If you are going to have good intentions, you should also have a good character. If you are plainly a bastard, then you might as well be honest about it and do everything for the wrong reasons. There is nothing worse, more damaging, than inconsistency.

To Hannah, a brother (Benedict). To Julius, a mistress, a son. To Evelyn, a daughter; a nice house in Frognal Road, Hampstead; a better-paid job with which to support everyone; a broadening of her mind, horizons, life. To Benedict, new toys as bribery.

It was Benedict, in fact, who blew the gaff and set the whole thing off. He could talk by now. He had learned from his mother, by example, to maintain an expression of innocence (I mean stupidity) in front of people. He had learnt the value of the artless question; the appeal of an expression of incomprehension; he had discovered how good it makes people feel if they think that they are doing you a favour. All the world loves a bimbo.

He opened his large eyes as he sat on Felix's knee and, just to see what would happen, he said, 'Why is Uncle Julius always trying to kiss my mummy?'

Wallop.

No, Felix didn't hit Benedict. He dropped Benedict to the floor and hit Evelyn. When Evelyn told me this story, she said that Felix was drunk and attacked her for no reason, and she tried to shield her baby boy from his blows. That wasn't what Benedict told me. In any case, Felix duffed Evelyn up, smashed the furniture a bit, taking care not to damage any of his paintings, and stormed out of the flat.

An hour later, Julius Drake zipped along in his little sports car. He had recently acquired this car to make up for his hair-loss. It was unfortunate for someone who liked to be as up to date as Julius did that, just as long hair became absolutely crucial, he lost most of his. In fact, he allowed all the hair around the sides of his head to grow long. But the effect wasn't what you might call aesthetic. Still, he had the sports car. He came bounding up the stairs to the studio with surprising energy for a man in his mid-thirties (but then, Julius always felt younger than he seemed), and found Evelyn in the distressed state already outlined.

He rescued her. She was butter in his hands. I find it almost impossible to try to explain to you why Evelyn left with Julius that day. Why she accepted him when she had rejected me. I suppose that she was trying to survive, trying to get the best for Benedict. It is particularly irritating that it was just at about this time I got my first well-paid job. I rented a nice house, and set off for Bristol to claim Evelyn, now that I had the wherewithal to support her. When I knocked at the flat the door was opened by another girl: a Chinese girl with doped eyes and a superior expression. She laughed when I asked for Evelyn. I have since learnt that laughter is the only emotion that the Chinese can express without losing face.

Evelyn thought about snipping the crotches out of Felix's trousers, but she thought that Julius might take the gesture amiss. Instead, she put Benedict in the Ferrari with all his toys, and told Julius to wait with him. Julius, seeing the glint of revenge in her eyes, made her promise not to damage any of the paintings (some of them were owed to him). That gave her an even better idea. There were three large nudes of herself in the studio. Felix had been dabbling in super-realism lately. The pictures had titles like 'Construction #32' and 'Still Life and the Wife'. Evelyn had hated being used for these paintings even more than being used for the abstracts. She painted three white cotton dresses on them. For the first time since she had moved in with Felix, she felt that her body was her own.

Julius had no trouble in finding her a job. He told her that, to be fair to herself, she should work. If they both earned money, they could have a fair and equal partnership. He took out a mortgage for half the value of the house in Frognal, and Evelyn gave him the equivalent of the payments in rent. I have never understood the logic of this convoluted procedure myself, but it shows the way his mind worked. He was always presenting her with long complicated calculations which, when they were boiled down, usually meant that she owed him money. I have had experience of this myself, on holiday with Julius. Being the accountant, he always did the adding and division of the restaurant bill and, by the time he had spent an hour entangling it, we would all have thrown our money on the table and left it to him. I think he usually had a free meal and made a profit, but it was never worth trying to argue with him. Besides, no one wanted to seem as mean as he did.

It was through Evelyn's new job that I met up with her again. She worked for a television company as a go-for on an arts programme. I was being interviewed as one of the new, well-paid revolutionaries of 1968. It was 1969 and already there was a sort of creepy nostalgia about the Sixties. That is what I didn't like about the Sixties. Everyone was so self-conscious, and trying so hard to be spontaneous and beautiful. People stayed awake all night trying to learn the new vocabulary and make their hair look as though it had never been washed. Everyone pretended to be eighteen years old and innocent and optimistic. That was fine if you were eighteen, but pretty rum when it was the balding Julius Drake clutching a Shasta daisy and humming with his eyes closed to levitate the Pentagon.

If Evelyn didn't recognise me straight away, it was because she was seeing me properly for the first time. She had just had her contact lenses fitted. She said that it was the most extraordinary experience she had ever had. The world was suddenly full of bright colours and defined shapes; things which people had spoken about for years and which she had never understood were suddenly clear to her. She spoke about her lenses the way most people spoke about LSD.

She asked me how I was and I told her that I was married. I wanted her to be hurt by this, but she seemed delighted; doubly delighted that it was Sally I was married to. She said she had always thought that we were meant for each other. It was me that was hurt and wounded, scraped on my patch of proud flesh. And I

31

was embarrassed to be seen by her. Already, my deterioration had begun. She was a new person and I was an old person.

Evelyn was a whole new person. She was more confident. She had lost a lot of her bimbo airs and wasn't afraid to make an intelligent remark in mixed company. Where once her eyes had been grey and mystified they were now the colour of walnut wood: yellow, golden and amber. Where her hair had once been sprayed into a single, even curve, it now hung back from her head in a wild mass of sprays and kinks and twists, as orange as God had intended. And she saw things that God had never intended her to see.

As well as her job and keeping house for Julius – and bringing up two small children – she had begun to educate herself. She was taking A levels by correspondence. She was about to enrol in the Open University for a degree in modern literature. Soon after I first saw her, she changed her job and began to work on one of the new game-shows. This exercise in entertaining the masses was probably some of the best training she ever had for her career as a writer. She learned what people expected and what people would put up with. She learned how to catch and hold people's attention.

Julius almost died when she told him about her new job. He recovered slightly when she told him that she would be earning more, but he still couldn't see how he could get around the shame of having a consort who involved herself in such a philistine occupation. He insisted that, when they went out to supper with artists and writers and publishers and, more especially, journalists, she should deny that she had a career at all. She was to say that she was just a mother.

She accepted this. I don't know if I can explain why to you. It was because, although Evelyn was a new person, Julius still treated and dealt with the old person. He spoke to her as though she was still the same set of goods that he had acquired in Clifton. He had bought her by raising her standard of life and her expectations just very slightly. He knew that, to make her happy, he would have to give her just a little more than Felix had. It wasn't his intention to liberate her. He didn't know that if he gave her an inch she would become this whole new person. And so, Julius saw no more than he expected to see, and he still treated Evelyn as though she was the idiot-child destitute that he had bargained for.

Evelyn gave Julius no reason to think otherwise. If she was treated as a bimbo, then she had no choice but to play the bimbo. It was an old comfortable role that she was used to, and, in a way, it was nice to slip back into it after a hard day of being a real person. Although she was already beginning to give the impression of superhumanity to the people around her, she had no feeling of being superhuman herself. She felt overworked and harrowed and frazzled and as though she was swimming very hard into the tide and getting nowhere. When Julius spoke to her sharply, or criticised her, she felt that he was the only one who had real insight into her character. That he knew the real her; the woman that was afraid and hiding behind a curtain of red hair. She was in the power of Julius. He could make her cry with one word, or even a look. He could order her to leave the house and she would sit, weeping on the doorstep with nowhere to go, hoping for his forgiveness, feeling her complete dependence on him. He ruled her by his cleverness and selfishness. By playing on her feelings of guilt and inadequacy. By his built-in feeling of male superiority and his professions of good intention. I know how he did it and why he did it because I have done it also. I should be contrite for this, but I don't think that Sally wanted or deserved anything better. Evelyn Cotton was different.

The house next door to Evelyn and Julius came up for sale and I bought it. It wasn't the cheapest place in London to buy a house at the time and I had to stretch myself financially to do it. But it was a compulsion. I thought that the house coming up for sale was fate screaming in my ear. If it was fate, then fate was taunting and goading me and laughing behind my back. To live beside Evelyn was a torture that was beyond me to resist.

1969, and there we all were in Frognal Road and denim hipsters. We were in and out of all those movements of the time as much as anyone else. I remember Evelyn and Sally going to Tufnell Park to see what all the feminist stuff was about, and coming back creased with mockery. Their impression was one of fierce women in kilts with an unhealthy interest in other women's sex lives. The feminist movement would have to wait another year or two before it could count Evelyn Cotton amongst its supporters. It was actually Sally who was stimulated into thought by the Tufnell Park Women's Group, and she went back on her own. It made me feel odd at times when I thought that she was standing up in front of other women and raising their consciousness by describing my oppression of her. Sex became peculiar at this time because I was never sure what she was going to tell them about at the next meeting, or whether she and her friends really wanted to castrate me. Luckily, she decided that lesbianism wasn't for her and I was saved the indignity of her running off with another woman.

Julius had done his stint at Haight-Ashbury, of course. He was right in there at just the crucial moment, but left Evelyn and the children to look after themselves. Not that their lives were impoverished by his absence. It was Evelyn's money that ran the household. She took a lover while he was away. Not me. I was disappointed, but disappointment was something I was learning to expect from Evelyn. If she had given me any signal at all that she needed a lover, I would have been there. But I never really thought of her as the adulterous type. Nor did I think that she had the time.

The first I knew of it was when she asked my advice about getting rid of him. It should have been a comfort to me that I was her best friend and the person she always turned to, but this I could have done without. The man was a creep: one of those sub-Che Guevara creatures who pretended to be workers fomenting revolution but who were really the sons of millionaire Mexican businessmen, attending English university at the expense of the starving peasantry of their homeland. Evelyn thought him attractive at first, but found herself becoming shy when he began to drop hints about S and M. This was the first of many lovers for Evelyn during her time with Julius. I always had the agony of being her agony aunt, and having to listen to the details. But she had no one else to talk to. Sally could only give answers in set pieces of diatribe. I hadn't yet introduced her to Sarah Bliss.

While Julius never suspected a thing about any of Evelyn's lovers, she was aware of every one of his. Poor Julius could never suppress anything. He was so self-concerned that he imagined a secret would stay secret of itself. It was peculiarly characteristic of him that he was unaware of his effect on people around him. He would go through a sleeping household at four in the morning, slamming doors on his way to the bathroom. But he had no idea

34

that he was making a noise, because he wasn't disturbing himself.

Evelyn didn't always confront him with her knowledge of these affairs. In the first instance, it would have been throwing stones from a glasshouse. Also, she was afraid that it would be the cue for him to suggest that they break up so that he could move in with the inamorata. She felt that her tenure with Julius was bound by delicate threads, and she still felt that she was dependent upon him. This has always been something of a mystery to me. It was she who made the money and it was she who looked after the children, and she had to look outside of her own household for love: but still she always believed that she was supported by Julius and that she needed him in order to exist. This belief carried right on into her life as an active feminist, when she was pretending to the general public that she knew better.

In a way, that has been Julius's supreme achievement. He has spent nearly twenty years of his life with the world's greatest feminist and managed to behave like a caveman; although he never expounded any but the soundest pro-feminist principles in public. I have often seen Evelyn return from a week of rousing the women of New Zealand to liberation, only to start straight in on a week's accumulated washing-up while Julius stormed about the house muttering and swearing to make her feel at home.

But we are still in 1969. The year is significant because it is the one in which Evelyn began to write. You may be forgiven for thinking that, behind the empire of thought that is Evelyn Cotton, there is the very worst sort of literary mogul, planning her media coverage and consulting the market forecasts before starting her next book. But you would be wrong. There is only Evelyn Cotton, her pencil and her copy book. When the telephone rings, she will answer it, and do her best to satisfy the person on the other end, be they battered wife or hack journalist.

She began to write her novels without ambition. It was a time when she needed a secret, a private activity to maintain her sanity. Her life was crowded out with the children, with Julius, lovers and a job. She got to the stage where it wasn't possible to go to the lavatory alone. If she was at work, she would have to tell her secretary where she would be. If she was at home, she would have to take a small, whimpering child with her, out of guilt for the poor, half-motherless thing. Julius sneered at her job one moment, and reminded her that they didn't have enough money the next. Progressive school fees didn't come from nowhere.

Julius Drake was a whisker away from the top of his pile. He had just been invited to make an entry in *Who's Who*. He had the gratitude and the respect of the English artistic community and was simultaneously acquiring a fortune. Even his parents were beginning to speak of him with some pride. When they died, in 1970, their hearts were intact and their intellectual honour was saved. After their death, Julius could have called himself a rich man, by anyone's standards. But he wasn't the sort of man who admitted to having money.

During the Sixties there were few flaws in his life. He had a biddable and conscientious wife (although he never had the grace to marry her) who was in full-time employment. He lived at the cultural centre of his society and allowed himself the freedom to travel at will, without his family. His clients were too unworldly to notice whose interests he was serving, and his collection of art and artefacts was beginning to look like the best in England, except that it was shown to no one.

None of this gave him any time to notice Evelyn. He stormed through her life, giving orders and muttering complaints, but rarely looked at her. One morning, as he was about to leave the house, as he was halfway out of the door, he stopped and gazed at Evelyn in a critical way, for what seemed a very long time. She was loading the dishwasher. As she became aware that he was watching her, her movements grew conscious and awkward. She knew that the shortness of her dress was unbecoming to her. She could feel his criticism pelting through the air.

He spoke in a sudden way, as though he had just comprehended the essentials of the problem and the best way of solving it. 'Evelyn, you are becoming fat,' he said. He closed the door behind him and drove away down the hills of Hampstead, dropping the children at their schools as he went. Evelyn stood, petrified, over the dishwasher, an egg-stained plate held in her two hands, afraid to move, lest she feel the bulk of which she had been accused or the scoring of elastic in her shoulder if she stretched. The weight of her breasts if she bent.

Tears fell on to the egg-stains, dripped from the plate into the machine and made the powder damp. She stood, immobilised and leaking for an hour, until her office called to know why she was late. She told them that she was ill. She did nothing for the rest of that day but weep. She lay awake that night thinking of nothing. She felt that she was waiting for something to come to her and bleed the misery out of her.

The next morning she rose from bed at a quarter past five, feeling that she had something to write down. There was nothing in her head, only a fear of herself as others might see her. She had nothing to say to anyone in the way of hope or condemnation; no thought in her mind for the women of the world, only an itch in her fingers.

She took an empty exercise book and a pencil stub from Benedict's school satchel. She crouched on the floor by the kitchen range and began her first novel. It was a novel about herself as she thought others saw her at the time. The subject was an odious, inadequate, miserable woman who was far too fat and whom nobody could love. She punished this woman for the body of the book, and then, feeling sorry for her at the end, vindicated her. It took seven months of early mornings in the kitchen to finish her work and, at the end of it, she felt better about herself and about her life; and she looked for no more from the experience.

She was one of the few people I have ever met who never said that there was a book in everyone, and who was never certain that her own life would make a bestseller. Perhaps she was without these vanities, or perhaps a real writer wouldn't say these things.

She put her manuscript into the back of the drawer and left it there until her life began to crowd in on her once more, and she felt that she must begin another. She rose again in the mornings and sat with her pencil stub, but nothing came out. Unable to understand what was wrong with her, she blamed the presence of the first manuscript which seemed to be seething in its drawer. She took the twenty-seven copy books out, and was about to throw them on the fire to be rid of them, when something stopped her. A compulsion came over her that the manuscript must be seen by another person before it could be destroyed. As she held the copy books over the range, she had the same feeling in her throat as when she booked the abortion for Felix's child.

Her secretary agreed to type up the manuscript. When the girl had finished, she refused payment. She said that the book had changed her, that she was grateful for being allowed to read it. Evelyn thought the response was odd, and that the secretary was perhaps in need of a holiday.

EVELYN HESITATED BEFORE sending the manuscript off to a publisher. She wasn't sure if she liked the idea of people going drippy because of what she had written. But the other book moved about inside her like an egg in a chicken, and she knew that there wasn't room for two unpublished manuscripts in one house. She had to get the first one out of the way so that she could get back to her secret scribbling, crouched by the range.

The moment was right. Her books were published and they made money. The tremors of feminism that had been crossing the Atlantic were beginning to seep through the public consciousness. Evelyn found herself written to and written about and admired and hated.

Still, Evelyn would not have called herself a feminist. She was not a person for joining movements. She liked to observe things without getting too closely involved. Sally, on the other hand, was up to her neck in it. It was she who would persuade Evelyn to come along and address women's meetings. One day, Sally and Evelyn were to meet for lunch. Sally was spending the day picketing outside Bow Street Magistrates' Court as a protest against the incarceration of feminists who had been arrested outside the Miss World Contest. Evelyn picked Sally up at one. She had nothing to do with the protest, but happened to have her photograph taken during the moment she was there. Her face was creased from a morning of high-pressure work and the worry of being surrounded by so many policemen. The photographer thought that, with her wild red hair, she looked like just the man-hating harpy he needed. A sub-editor recognised her face, and the photograph of Evelyn was published across the front page of the *Observer* with her name below it and a headline above it which read 'WOMEN'S LIB: COULD IT HAPPEN HERE?'.

Whether she liked it or not, Evelyn had become a feminist. Once she had been pushed across the line, she began to see the legitimacy of the movement. The truths of women's oppression were too self-evident to be denied. But still, because she hadn't been enrolled of her own free will, there was no question of her applying the principles of sisterhood to her own life. The line between her two existences became more defined. In front of the world she was frighteningly intelligent; the champion of the downtrodden. Her opinion of every issue was canvassed and published. The most respectable arts programmes reviewed and praised her work. Thousands waited to read her next novel, and women in every country of the world changed their lives through the influence of her writing.

But, to Julius, she was still the same good-natured girl he had brought from Clifton in his Ferrari. He was slightly puzzled by her success, and couldn't understand what the fuss was about. He could see that her books were not great literature. Great literature, to Julius, was something that was inside of himself; something the world was still waiting for. There were times when he wondered if he and Evelyn had been drawn towards each other because they were both writers. But he was rarely as generous as this to Evelyn. More often, he thought that she was feeding off his genius. That her (inferior) talent was due to her proximity to him.

It wasn't easy for Julius to be addressed as Mr Cotton. When people were kind enough to attend to him for a moment and ask him what he did, he would say that he was an accountant, and then watch as their expression glazed and they changed the subject by asking him what Evelyn was like at home.

At home, nothing had changed.

As that dreary decade, the Seventies, clicked over, Evelyn and Julius, like that barometer couple who come in and out to indicate the weather, slowly changed places. When Julius reviewed his life and counted his blessings in 1970, he had a lot to be smug about (smugness is a thing which Julius suffers from). He was wealthy;

his adultery-level was above average; he was in control of his home life; and, beyond all this, he had yet to embark on his world-scorching, Nobel prize-winning literary career. Is it surprising to us that someone who had so carefully nurtured and controlled his life should so seriously underestimate the Fates?

As Evelyn Cotton, through accident and justice, ascended through the Seventies; as acolytes and journalists came to camp in her garden; as her confidence increased and she began to give the opinions she was asked for: so Julius Drake went to the bad. His life, as he had planned it, fell asunder; and he was left to scheme a new one.

But a lot of this can only be seen with hindsight. Nobody ever seemed to know where they were going. Our lives in Frognal Road seemed very ordinary to us. Drab and unglamorous. I find it hard to remember events or incidents from the Seventies. It is as though one spent those ten years asleep in a coffin of fudge. The children got bigger. Sally grew older. Clothing became less of an embarrassment. There were some moments that were halted by the camera before they merged with the general fog. Perhaps I have no memory of the Seventies at all. I only know what I have seen in photographs. I have constructed an artificial memory from these happysnaps.

Perhaps that is why I sometimes think that we spent most of the Seventies on holiday. The only evidence that we existed at all in those ten years shows us on beaches and mountains, sunburnt, disgruntled and determined to enjoy, but always feeling slightly cheated.

There is one holiday that represents the whole of the decade to me. It was the nine of us, as so many holidays were. Evelyn, Julius, Benedict, Hannah, Sally, Our Three, and me. We rented a villa in the south-west of France. It was an idyllic, a wonderful place: a private garden with swags of flowering creepers.

I proposed shopping on the first morning, but only the children were willing to come into the town with me. Sally and Evelyn said that they wanted to rest. Julius was allergic to the possibility of spent money. We had a nice time in the town. Benedict was a boy of twelve with skinny legs and big, bony knees, like a famine child. He was reserved, and apt to sulk but, if you knew him, you could see that somewhere inside his head he was observing us all, and laughing to himself. Hannah and my own children were quite ordinary. We ate ice-creams and apricot tarts and smiled because of the heat of the sun. I remember the happiness of that first morning because of the contrast between it and the rest of the holiday.

We got back to find Evelyn, Sally and Julius all sunbathing nude in the garden. I didn't know where to put myself, and I think that the children were just as embarrassed. That was the thing about the Seventies: it was blasphemy to suggest that there could be such a thing as indecency. You had to go along with whatever everyone was doing, no matter how revolting. The children and I stammered and shuffled around. The sunbathers looked up at us, lazy and self-satisfied, and said wasn't it glorious.

The children spent that holiday in large jerseys and long trousers. They were paler at the end than at the beginning, but with a slight, overheated flush to their cheeks, as though they were consumptive. From their reaction, I felt that, if I took my clothes off, I would be betraying them, so I spent my holiday reading novels in the shade of the verandah. It was a difficult time for me: Evelyn lolling about ten yards away, as often as not with her legs parted and her fanny pointed at me; me, pretending to read, but, from behind sunglasses, able to study every fold of skin and strand of hair. I knew what it was to be Tantalus. I wanted nothing more than to make my whole self small and crawl inside of her. Instead, I had a job disguising the parts of me that were made big by the sight of her. I sat in the shade, in loose clothing, permanently on the boil. This meant that I had to trouble Sally four or five times a day and, by the end of the holiday, I was physically as well as mentally banjaxed.

And with all this there was the shame of my wife not caring that everyone should see what a lumpy, hirsute woman she was. The shame of people thinking that I wasn't going to undress because I was ashamed of my pot belly and my hairy back and my mean, flabby arms. I had already deteriorated quite a lot by then. I was old before my time and, although I wasn't fat, although the rest of my body was normal, I had this lump, this cancer – this swelling, black with hair – that dominated the middle of my body.

Perhaps the worst of it was to have Julius's ghastly thing constantly dangled before me with the same taunting smugness that its owner displayed. Of having to hold polite conversations with Julius as he stood around me, playing the natural, unstrung, hung-out groover. As Evelyn and Julius went to bed at night, I felt as the Irish peasantry of the 1840s must have felt when they watched their grain go to the English.

For what it is worth, that holiday is how I remember the Seventies. I was too old to be aware of Johnny Rotten, and I worked too hard to be political. Before we knew where we were, Thatcher came to power, and the Eighties were here and money was talked about as the prime motivation. Perhaps that makes this age more honest than any other.

You would think that Julius would be suited to a Thatcherite environment but, really, he was dependent on the old system. For Julius to operate, he needed to be the only one that knew anything about money. When all those people who had never involved themselves with money before bought stocks and shares, and investors began to turn to art to sink their excess fortunes and gain credibility, the climate which had made Julius's enterprise a success disappeared. It was no longer fashionable to be unworldly, and people began to discuss the merits of their accountants openly at dinner; people began to notice that they were getting a raw deal from Julius.

His clients noticed that they sometimes paid more income tax than their gross earnings. Julius was slipping. His heart was no longer in it. Even to the unworldly, it began to seem as though they should look for a new financial manager. The paintings which they had given to Julius in the Sixties were now worth small fortunes, and Julius's services could no longer be called a bargain. The clients with courage began to drop him. He ranted and screamed at them and called them ungrateful traitors, and usually refused to return any of their documents. He acquired the reputation for being even worse as an enemy than he was as a friend, and the most timid people remained as his clients rather than face up to him.

Julius tried not to be outdated. He had his hair cut short and affected country clothing. But he knew that his only hope for survival lay in a complete change of life, away from the new school of sleek money-eaters. With Evelyn in the ascendant and himself in decline he would achieve nothing. He knew that there would have to be a big shuffle to put things back the way they should be.

His old fantasies of being the Grand Man of English Letters began to hover before him. Julius had, so far in his life, failed to produce one paragraph of literature. He held a conviction that this negligence was due entirely to his environment. He knew that he could never write so long as he lived in a city.

This man who, apart from his prolonged moment at Haight-Ashbury and a small perambulation in the vicinity of Kathmandu, had spent his entire life, not only in the city of London but in the same part of London; moving from a childhood in Hampstead to a youth in Camden, to a prosperity back in Hampstead; who was afraid of dogs and cattle; who strode around Cornwall with a thumbstick and cap (to the intense embarrassment of everyone in his company); who wouldn't know a sheep from a stoat: this man possessed an enduring fantasy that if he moved to the mythical English countryside and lived an idyll, a great twentieth-century novel would come pouring from his tortured soul. Prose for the world to remember him by.

It is possible that we all want to be remembered by posterity, but not all of us, ultimately, expect it. Within the stout walls of his ego, Julius was convinced of his place in history. He was assured by every fibre of his selfishness that he was a towering figure, and that the world only needed to be made to look up in order to see him.

What he needed first was a setting that was grand enough to contain the grandeur of his ideas: a house that matched and reflected his image of himself; that represented him as he believed others should see him.

This house was to be in a countryside that neither you nor I have ever seen. The sort of place that features in advertisements for muesli or shampoo: swags of blossom hanging from apple trees that are coincidentally bending with fruit; haywains and old roses and Jersey cattle with clean hocks. This countryside was to have a population whose only function was the maintenance of the picturesque (but which contained the odd eccentric, charming scruff who knew how to keep his place).

Evelyn Cotton who, like me, had been born and reared in the real countryside, and whose relations lived in daily fear of banks foreclosing on farm loans; who had been a child at a time when there really was a countryside, and not the thinly disguised suburb it is today, felt justified in thinking that she actually knew something about country life. She blamed the country for the repression and backwardness of her youth, and for the early mistakes of her life. Rather than as a representation of freedom, with its vast expanses of empty land, she saw the country as a socially claustrophobic place, full of bucolic, ignorant, bored people where nothing real could ever be achieved. She thanked London for what freedom and independence she had; for lovers discreetly gained and lost; for her meteoric career as a writer. She knew that she needed to stay in London if she was to maintain the person she had become. Julius knew that she would never willingly leave it.

Although he was completely aware of her abhorrence of a country life, Julius gave no more credence to her opinions in this than in anything else. Once he had decided that the country was where they must live, he embarked upon a wily and carefully conceived campaign to win her agreement.

I never knew why Julius didn't just leave London and Evelyn and Benedict and go to live in an Alison Uttley illustration all by himself. He may, I suppose, have loved her, although I find this hard to believe. After years of close observation of Julius, I decided that he was incapable of love; incapable of any emotion which involved giving anything away. He suffered from infatuation from time to time, and he would take me out for a drink and behave in an agonisingly smug manner while he bombarded me with hints about his latest sordid conquest. (Except, of course, when he had an affair with Sally, and Sally broke down and confessed it to me. I threw her out of the house, but she instantly came back with Julius *and* Evelyn, and we had to sit up until five in the morning talking it through and raising our consciousness, everyone patronising me as though it was my problem in the first place. I told Julius that if he wanted the bitch, I would swop her for Evelyn. Evelyn was suffocated by giggles for a moment which she disguised as a coughing fit – I think she found the whole thing as ludicrous as I did – and everyone said I had a right to be upset, and that I should go with my feelings. In the Seventies, they even took the pleasure out of losing your temper.)

So, let us consider that Julius didn't love Evelyn. There are other reasons for wanting to be with someone. She supported the household; indeed, as her accountant, Julius made a profit out of her. She was past master at cooking the sort of food which Julius liked to eat: what anyone else would call economical cookery; pumpkin pie and lentil soup. She was a companion to whom he had grown accustomed. His daughter loved her as a mother. He would be bound to lose something in a separation; have to replace some of the saucepans or the washing machine. Julius hated to lose anything. He had been keeping cake and eating it all of his life. He was rotten with kept cake. Evelyn, as a part of his cake collection, would have to accompany him to the country.

It may seem to you that I am only presenting one side of Julius's character. You may look with some scepticism at my list of his reasons for wanting to keep Evelyn by him. All I can say is that I had to live beside him, you didn't.

His campaign of persuasion began by telling her that her tax position was delicate. He filled his reasoning with technical jargon, the way he always did when it came to money. They were in the room that she used as an office. She was at her desk, looking abstractedly through the window and beyond into the garden. He was swinging on the handles of the open door, his head between his raised shoulders, like a resting vulture. He had become an excessively thin creature in recent years; nervous in his movement and sly in his speech. He looked ten years older than he was.

This scene was familiar to me. I could see into Evelyn's office from our kitchen. Evelyn would sit at her desk looking well and unworried. Her right hand would scribble with the pencil. Her face would be so placid as to make you think she was in a trance. Is placid the right word? I don't mean complacency or that sort of bovine immobility; I mean something that is closer to the tranquillity of a cat. Evelyn is feline in a lot of ways. She glides rather than walks. Her eyes are the same shade of yellow: copper in some lights; tinged with green in others.

Now she is sitting at her desk and is surrounded by her cats. The cats are unsettled by Julius's presence. One by one, they slide from the desk and shoot past him, out of harm's way. Julius is speaking to the back of Evelyn's head, and so her eyes and expression are invisible to him. He is talking about tax and money and net and gross and higher rate less exemption. He might as well be talking about the fish market prices. She doesn't know why he is bothering. She leaves everything financial to him. She signs what is put in front of her. She believes herself to be useless with money and feels guilty about the amount she spends. If Julius says that they are in financial difficulty, not only will she believe it, but she is prepared to believe that it is her fault. Her guilt centres around her Harrods account, which is the only bill he never asks to see. Her reaction to this fiscal lecture is to kick off her new shoes beneath her desk and fold her arms to hide the bracelets.

He sighs impatiently, as if he is indulging her stupidity.

'You don't seem to understand.' He speaks to her slowly, as if she has no brain, this woman consulted by the brains of Europe. But Julius Drake knows her better.

She can see that it is time to pay attention; that he won't go away for being ignored. She turns around to stare at him. 'If we need more money, then I had better do that terrible television thing.'

'You won't understand. What I am saying is that you may have to become a tax exile. We might have to go and live in Jersey or Ireland, or perhaps the Isle of Man.'

(It should be said here that Julius had no intention of moving to these places. But this reasoning was that, if you want to make someone do something they won't like, you propose something that they will like less. Then the thing that you wanted in the first place seems innocuous by comparison. The more complicated and befogged the problem is, the more relieved and grateful your subject will be when you present a comparatively painless solution.)

The horror and discomfort on Evelyn's face fell nicely into his projections. The prospect of having to leave her beloved London stirred Evelyn from her placidity. She squawked, 'A tax exile? I can't become a tax exile. What about my life?'

'What about your life?'

'My children? My writing? My friends? It is stupid to say that I should give everything up because I am earning too much money. It is immoral. If that is the case, I will earn less. I will write slower.'

She snapped her pencil in two, symbolically. Julius winced at the waste of it.

'You can't understand. Nothing is as simple as that. It will take everything you can earn this year, and more, to pay your taxes. And

47

how will you pay the tax on that? You have no option. You are not in a bracket that can afford to live in a country like this.'

'I thought the whole point of Thatcher was that I was. I understood that money was being snatched from the mouths of orphans and opera houses to subsidise people like me.' She was angry with him for a moment.

'What are you saying? Are you saying that I made this up? That I came in here to tell you that you are up to your neck in taxes for a joke?'

'I'm sorry,' she said.

'It doesn't have to be as bad as you think. We can pay the taxes by selling this house. Then, if we move somewhere for a while where you are tax-free, we will be ahead of ourselves again. I've gone through all the options and there isn't another way. There are lots of writers living in Ireland now.'

'Rotting in Ireland, do you mean?' Her voice still had traces of her anger; of her disturbance, but she was trying to be good; to be a sensible girl for Julius. 'And so, even so, even if we sell this house, if we move to the middle of a wild bog with no neighbours, if there is no money, how will we buy a house to live in?'

'Property is cheap in Ireland,' he said.

'Houses that are worth living in are never cheap. Comfort has always to be paid for. I don't earn this much just to live in a hovel.'

'Just think about it for a while,' he said, as he made to leave the room. He considered that his first nail was well driven home.

'No, wait! Can't we just mortgage this house and go on living in it? Can't we do something else? Why is this so sudden? Couldn't you just lend me the money? Couldn't the bank?'

Her voice brought him back from halfway out of the door. He tried an expression of injury, but he couldn't, somehow, fit it to his face. He creased his features into goodness and patronising sympathy instead.

'Can't you believe me? You know that I have no money I can touch. You know that, if it was possible for me to give you the money, it would be the first thing I would suggest. I don't want to leave here any more than you. This has been my home for longer. It kills me to think of selling this house. I told you often enough in the past that you should have been putting money by for a time like this, instead of spending it like water. I have tried to hold all of this together for as long as I could. We have to sell. I went to the bank.

I have tried for a mortgage. Can't you just do one thing to help, and trust me, instead of throwing obstacles in my path?'

He had floored her before he had finished speaking. The first glaze of tears was forming over her contact lenses. It took him a bit longer these days than it used to, to poke at her guilt and feelings of inadequacy until she wept. It used to take only one carefully chosen remark. Now it needed a long paragraph. But you had to have tears before you could hope for a reconciliation, and you couldn't win without reconciliation. He was smiling at her now. The smile was meant to convey his forgiveness of her. That is how she interpreted this smile of his. You or I might interpret it differently.

Julius Drake has the most peculiar smile. When he wears it, he is often mistaken for an undertaker. Partly, because he has no lips. Partly, because smiling is unnatural to him. Partly, because it is really a sort of smirk. His mouth forms a kind of U-shape while remaining tightly closed. His eyes still dart about suspiciously. The bottom half of his face looks exceptionally pleased with itself. The top half looks as though it were about to be hit. The effect is to make you want to hit him.

We are getting ahead of ourselves. Everyone will have the chance to take a good swing at Julius in time.

Evelyn, meantime, with her tears only just in check, is more or less where Julius wants her. If she is upset, then it must be that she accepts what he has told her. She said, 'And so. If we sell this house. Will it be enough?'

'Yes,' he said, kindly but firmly. He had only just stopped himself from saying, 'Your half will.' He began to wonder if he was obliged to give her any of it at all. He would call his solicitor next day. In any case, dividing property could be left for another time. For now, they must appear to be fighting something together. He said something reassuring to her, something that she hardly heard, and then he left her to herself.

That first interview was to be almost the easiest he had with her on the subject of their leaving London. She wasn't that stupid, our Evelyn. And by the time she had talked to me and the likes of Sarah Bliss, there were a few pertinent questions she had to ask of Julius. Sarah and I were always steering Evelyn away from precipices. Her trouble was that, because she was so kind, she

49

expected other people to be acting from the same motives. She was willing to believe people, by and large.

But whatever flaws she saw in Julius's propositions, he always had his answer. They both felt that their survivals were at stake. Why didn't they just split up there and then, and try to survive on their own like civilised adults? Perhaps there is no such thing as a civilised adult. It may even be a contradiction in terms.

Evelyn raged at Julius from time to time. But afterwards she would feel guilty because she saw him only as the bearer of bad news, and he had convinced her that she herself was the source of the evil.

She had made as much money in the previous ten years as any serious writer could hope for. She had spent it before it was made. She had bought and mortgaged a house for her mother; she had financed her brother in various schemes; had educated, clothed and fed her own child and Julius's child without making fish of one and flesh of the other; had run the household and paid the bills and the daily woman and a part-time secretary who seemed to mostly work on Julius's behalf, and paid her own way in restaurants, and taken them all – and half their friends – on holiday. She had done all of this with so little consciousness of the money leaving her hands that, if you asked her where it all went, she would look as guilty as a cat in the fridge, and hide her new shoes and say in a tremulous voice beneath her breath something about supposing it must be the Harrods account.

Julius, on the other hand, always seemed to be in the throes of a financial crisis whenever a final demand came skidding down the hall. He also held himself to be morally above money because his clients paid him with work rather than cash. Because she could have no idea how much he was worth, and because he always said so, Evelyn assumed that he had nothing. She knew that his parents must have left him money, but he vaguely gave out that it had all been swallowed by debts, and she found that she could sympathise with this. Sometimes, when she could be bothered to think about it, she wondered how someone as mean as Julius could profess not to care about money. But, most of the time, she was running to meet the demands of her own harrying bank manager. She has been called a prolific writer. The credit for this is perhaps due to Mr Blomfield at the bank.

Although she knew nothing about Julius's finances, he, as her accountant, was intimate with every decimal point of hers. He charged her a fee for his services, but always made sure that he left her with enough to meet the bills. This tax bill which he now flourished had some basis in fact, but it was no more than the tax bill which had appeared every year since Evelyn's success. On other occasions, he had appealed it and fiddled and whittled it down to a manageable figure, but this year he had other uses for it.

He persuaded her to go househunting in Ireland with him. Time spent doing a reconnaissance, he said, was never time wasted. He had relations settled in County Waterford, and so the cost of the trip would be negligible. A little holiday.

They went when the weather was bad. They left a crisp and snowy England and arrived in an Ireland up to her knees in mud. Julius's relation was in the depths of a neurotic depression. Her husband was permanently drunk. They borrowed money from Evelyn and told her that she must be mad to want to live in Ireland. They hated it and would escape if they could. Julius smirked and said that they were like that wherever they lived.

Julius and Evelyn spent half a morning in a cold estate agent's office in Dungarven, waiting for the agent to return from a funeral. When he arrived he was obsequious and smarmy. They could have done without a further twenty minutes of his strong-smelling apologies. He brought them to see houses: the sort of large romantic places he thought they would like and no one else would buy. They were, without exception, leaky, mouldy and unheated. When Evelyn's foot went right through a floorboard she said she would like to go home. But, first, they had to stand through a further half-hour of creeping wellwishing and apologies.

Evelyn refused to spend another night in Ireland. They caught the evening ferry back to England. They had dinner on the boat, a disgusting meal of fishfingers and chips which had been advertised as Goujons of Plaice on the menu. Evelyn had been taciturn all day. When the waiter told her that there was no fresh black pepper on the boat, she finally broke.

'I will scrub floors. I will go to prison for my taxes. I am not moving to Ireland. I will die first.'

Julius said, 'But, my darling, dreadful circumstances have

always been conducive to great literature. Despair makes good art. Ireland could see the flowering of your misery.'

'Balls,' said Evelyn in a loud voice.

Julius and the waiters were horrified. Evelyn's normal voice was barely a whisper. Her tone was one of persuasive suggestion. She seduced you into close attention to what she had to say. This last exclamation was out of character.

There was nothing more Julius could say. Although he had won his point, he felt slightly out of his depth with this new, violent Evelyn. For a moment, she reminded him of his father, and that was not a happy memory. Her face had an unstable, swelling expression, like that of a pneumatic tyre about to explode. Normally, he could depend on her to ease into a trickle of tears with barely a change of demeanour. Now, he sensed a volcanic aspect to her character which was new to him. He withdrew his head like a tortoise, and studied his Goujons of Plaice from between his shoulders.

They came all the way back to London in utter silence: Evelyn thinking that they were in an irredeemable fix; and Julius quietly polishing the details of the next stage in his plan.

So far, he had been successful. The need to leave London seemed to be fixed in her mind, and she had accepted that the London house was to be sold. He had adroitly seen to it that she was persuaded of the horrors of living in tax havens, and so it seemed to be the time to present a lesser evil.

The next move was to prove to her the charm of the English countryside as quickly as possible, before she became aware of any other possibilities. The cleverest of their friends at that moment were selling their Hampstead houses for large sums of money and moving to south and east London at a considerable profit. These were the days just before the yuppie boom and Evelyn's finger was too much on the pulse of the nation for Julius's comfort. He had to establish in her mind the fact that they were moving to the country as soon as he could, without making it seem that it was what he himself wanted to do.

He suggested that they spend a weekend with their friends, the Bennets, in Somerset. Evelyn agreed. There was no reason why she shouldn't. The Bennets had been inviting them for years. Indeed, the Bennets had been the most regular occupants of the spare room in Hampstead since 1965. A weekend with the Bennets in Somerset was inevitable at some point. Julius saw that it could have its advantages now.

Shall we talk Bennet first, so that you know who they are? I think we should, as the Bennets fall into that category of people who are far more interesting to talk about than they are to talk to.

Ned Bennet is a painter. Hilda is an interior designer. Ned has always despised her profession, and Hilda has always supported his. Not only was Hilda the only earner in the household, but Hilda's various clients were the only people ever known to buy Ned Bennet's paintings. A Hilda Bennet interior is immediately recognisable by the garish, semi-abstract representations of fresh offal and decomposing women.

Physically, Ned is large and coarse, and Hilda is small and simpering. Ned gave out that he had a large libido by pinching a lot of bottoms, the larger the more, and rolling his eyes at strange women. But he was always saved from disgrace, or vindication, by his own hideousness. It was unlikely that any self-respecting woman would associate herself with so unbecoming a personage, and impossible that she would admit the affair if she had.

Hilda Bennet bore her husband's public incontinence with a milder hysteria than might be expected. She was a great one for talking things through with anyone that might listen. She held herself to be a very understanding person and to be in possession of an innocent mind. She made a point of not only believing any half-cocked psychological excuses he threw at her, but of repeating them to her friends for advice and comfort. So, when Ned explained his impotence to her by saying that any man past the age of twenty-eight is incapable of showing physical interest more than once a month (unless outrageously stimulated), she grasped at his straw, and spread her new knowledge among her friends so that they could have a better understanding of their own marriages.

This was not what Ned had intended. He didn't mean her to actually believe him. He wanted her to think that he was being stimulated elsewhere, and to grudgingly accept his excuse rather than jeopardise their marriage. Ned imagined himself as the hero of a work by Henry Miller, and that is how he wanted the world and his wife to imagine him. Hilda's faith in him forced him to invent affairs. He would spend long hours in gloomy public houses by himself and return to her, saying, as unconvincingly as he could, that the car had broken down.

But, far from suspecting a straying virility, Hilda brought her commendable understanding and innocence to bear. She always kindly offered to pay his garage bills and made him hot soup, and counted the days until her once in a month when he might be reliably counted on to seduce her in a spontaneous manner.

So much for the Bennets among themselves. To those who had a slight acquaintance with them, they were tedious people. To their close friends and their oldest friends, they were tolerable subjects for conversation and willing participants in any social catastrophe. Ned's chief interest in life was, in fact, to be an agent of chaos. If a crack appeared in your life, you could depend on Ned to rip it open. He was known as a stirrer. Hilda, on the other hand, was a great mender of fences. We will see them both at full stretch later.

Meanwhile, Evelyn and Julius were about to visit them:

It was a warm, fresh spring weekend, at about the turn of the fiscal year. Daffodils frittered on the hillsides and fritillaries danced in the meadows. Country cottages peered coyly from the windows of the better estate agents. The Bennets, in a coy cottage of their own – the ultimate expression of Hilda's art, were on their best behaviour. They lit bright fires to make the rooms seem cheerful and turned the heating up to make it seem warmer.

When the Londoners arrived, the full moon had just been and gone, and Ned had proved himself to the satisfaction of both the Bennets; and so, the atmosphere was all smoothness and contentment. Julius felt that the gods were with him in the enterprise.

'How interesting,' he remarked to Evelyn in private, 'that the Bennets, who always seem to be fighting in London, should seem so happy at home. In the country.'

The country itself was in a deceptive mood. All that weekend it wore full make-up. The weather was perfect; no farmer, from what they could smell, spread pig manure, and all was verdure and tranquillity. Evelyn, recently flogged to death by a lecture tour of Canada, found herself rested and relaxed. On the Sunday night, when she was sleepy, happy and lulled to abstraction, Julius said to her, 'Do you think, it has occurred to me; I don't know if it is possible, that we could be as settled and happy as Ned and Hilda if we could find a way of moving to the country?'

'I don't know,' she murmered, not having fully taken in what he was saying. They had had a late lunch of fresh lamb and good red wine. The effect was narcotic, and Evelyn was far away.

Julius pressed his point. 'It seems: it just seems that most of our troubles, a lot of the problems we have had: how can anyone be contented in London?'

Julius knew exactly what he was doing. He was suggesting things to Evelyn as a hypnotist would. He knew that, in her present state, she was open to such suggestion. Because she worked so hard, it was rare these days to see her so relaxed. He pursued his advantage.

'These days, we seem to just quarrel and spend money. There's no quiet, no time to be by ourselves. All of our problems and having to sell the house seem to come from living in London. Perhaps we should try the country. Certainly, it would go a long way to solving your problems. My business would suffer. I can see that. But it seems more important that we survive. It seems a long time since we have been as happy as we are this weekend. We could muddle through. I'm sure we could. It could mean not having to go abroad. I would have to give a lot of things up but, at least, we would be happy.'

He rattled on, possessed with himself and believing that he was imprinting his will on her brain. In the old days, he might have.

Evelyn was no longer dozing. Although everything seemed the same to Julius, and outside the balmy spring afternoon was darkening and the lambs were calling for their mamas and from the kitchen was coming the gentle click and drip of the Bennets loading the dishwasher together, and Evelyn seemed to be in the same position with her eyes shut and her left hand moving in the fur of the cat, playing the purr of the creature like an instrument – although Julius was rattling on, he had just lost his cause with Evelyn.

Somewhere, the monotonous whinge of his voice had stopped ringing true for her. She began to distance herself from what he said, and she found what he was saying impossible to believe. She almost laughed out loud when he became self-sacrificial, but chose to go on with her listening. That was the moment she braced herself for a life of her own.

It is not true that this was Evelyn's first clear and distanced glimpse of the real Julius. They had been together for fifteen years. There had been times, in the Sixties, when he had thrown her out of the house, and left her wailing on the doorstep. Unless you are very stupid, it is difficult to live with someone for that length of time and be unaware of what they are capable of. This knowledge, this suspicion, however, is generally lost in the complication of keeping things going from day to day. What happened here, in the Bennet's sitting-room, was that, as Julius twittered on in a voice that was naturally unattractive, to a background chorus of bleating lambs (made surreal because of having consumed one of their species), Evelyn's abstract suspicions of him came to her all at once. For the first time, he struck her as being completely despicable: he was no longer an everyday faulted character of rather ordinary magnitude.

She became aware of the pressure of him herding her into a position that was favourable to himself. She had no idea what he wanted her to do, or of his motives for wanting it, but she could see, at last, that he was operating a gameplan which he had structured, and which he had initiated.

Evelyn and the cat, in the same armchair; in the same state of half sleep and complete alertness. Their yellow eyes almost closed and their ears strained for sound. If Evelyn and the cat had nearly everything in common, the exception was this: that the cat would always preserve itself first; Evelyn, being a writer, would feel compelled to stay and observe the minutiae of her own destruction.

Although Julius is discovered, she will allow him to go on out of curiosity. She will resolve and mean to do something to save herself, but will remain fascinated and inactive.

Already in her mind, she is planning a book about manipulative, overbearing men, even before Julius has finished his monologue.

THE NEXT DAY, they left for London in the middle of the morning. As they passed through Warminster, Julius stopped the car outside an estate agency. He said it was just to see, and out of interest. Evelyn waited in the car. She had an afternoon of television people to prepare her mind for. She had a pain in the small of her back, and she was not in the mood for indulging Julius.

Earlier that morning, with a critical attitude towards him which seemed new to her, she had observed him closely. Perhaps she was researching the new book. If someone is to stand up to the closest scrutiny, then you need to be in love with them not to be disgusted. Personal habits and small failings have to be glazed with charm in order to be borne. I think I can say with some certainty, from the way Evelyn reacted to her observation, that she was not in love with Julius.

There were all the usual things: the picking of toes; noises from the lavatory; the undefended physiognomy of a sleeper. The average human is an undeniably revolting thing. Imagine, then, waking up next to Julius Drake of a morning.

As she told it to me afterwards, the thing that really put her off Julius was his manner of eating. She had always been slightly embarrassed by his table manners, but usually had to think about what was on her own plate, or attend to the manners of the children. Now, she sat back, with her food untouched, and watched him make a pig of himself. She was horrified. He shovelled in food. He snatched, and he left his mouth open. She was sure that his manners couldn't have been like this when she met him.

The Bennets hardly batted an eyelid. Ned Bennet, for all his boorishness, ate like a dainty courtier. Hilda was so refined that she never ate at all in front of other people, although the lumpishness of her figure testified to substantial eating in private. Evelyn stayed transfixed, mesmerised by the sucking noises from his open mouth, as Julius held forth on the righteousness of socialism and modern architecture.

Evelyn sat in the car and wished for the day to be over. She wanted to be back in her own house, in her own office, in her own company. Meanwhile, Julius was farting about in Warminster.

When he returned to the car, he was overanimated. His face bobbed up and down outside her window as he signalled for her to open it. He was too agitated to notice the expression of horror he drew from her. She wound her window down.

'Come and see, come and see,' he said, jittering on the pavement.

'I am going to be late,' she said. 'What is it?'

'You won't be late. Not very late. They can wait for you. They usually have to. Just for a minute. Come and see.'

He was in too much of a dither to be argued with, so she followed him into the shop where he scuttled about like a spider in a bathtub. He showed her all the coy cottages pasted up, while he stood, first on one leg and then on the other, drawing her into corners and speaking out of the side of his mouth in a stage hiss, so that the assistant wouldn't be aware that they were interested in anything. Evelyn tried to give the assistant the odd reassuring smile, and the assistant, for his part, smiled back with a perfect, though condescending, understanding.

Julius began to prate in earnest volubility, once they were back in the car. Evelyn, aware of the artificiality of it all, began to lose her temper.

'My God,' Julius said, 'why did we never think of it before? It is such an obvious thing. If we sold the house in Hampstead, half of it would pay the taxes, the other half would buy the most wonderful cottage. You would have somewhere peaceful to write. We could be free of debt, free of all the problems we ever had. We don't need that big house, now that the children will be at university all the time.'

'For Christ's sake,' she suddenly shouted, cutting through all his banter. 'Do you have to drive so bloody fast?'

She shocked him. He thought he had her in the palm of his hand. Now her crossness made him cross. He snapped, 'I thought you were afraid of being late.'

She snapped, 'I'd rather be late than dead, if you don't mind.'

He snapped, 'Well, perhaps you would like to learn to drive.'

She snapped, 'It would be fine if you hadn't spent an hour twittering in Warminster.'

He yelled, 'I like that. That's just fine. I am trying to straighten *your* life out. Solve *your* problems. Pay *your* debts. Perhaps I just shouldn't bother.'

She screamed, 'Well, perhaps you shouldn't. If you were half an accountant, I shouldn't be in this mess in the first place. Why should I have to move to some boghole, just because you are an incompetent?'

He bawled, 'How dare you? You think I actually want to give up my work and my friends. I have been trying to make things easy for you. If you didn't spend half your life in Harrods, none of this would be happening.'

That was it. He had said the last thing. The thing that should be kept in reserve. She said in a calm voice, 'Stop the car. I am getting out.'

He did. She got out. He roared away, thinking that a walk would teach her gratitude. She marched to the nearest house and telephoned for a taxi.

You might think that was it. You might think that the taxi fare from Wiltshire to London would throw cold water on any scheme. Not in Julius's case. By the time Evelyn had caught up with him, he had worked it all out from the beginning again. He had filled her office with flowers, he had paid Benedict's outstanding school fees, he had bought a take-away supper to save her from cooking. She was too exhausted to do anything but accept.

From that time, she realised that his obsession with moving to the country was greater than she had the power to counteract. Julius spoke about it to their friends so that, when she met them, they exclaimed, 'So, you are moving to the country. When? Whatever for?'

She knew the answer to neither question, and hadn't time nor energy to work it out. Through lack of ammunition to destroy it, she allowed the fact to become established and accepted.

She felt that her resistance could be passive, as long as the danger was not immediate. They still lived in London, and she was grateful for this. Julius hadn't yet specified the object of their move, and so the move was an abstract idea. There was no new house or village to object to; to rail against.

She was grateful, too, that Julius, by some financial wizardry, seemed to have organised it so that selling the London house wasn't quite as urgent as it had seemed. She still had no suspicion that her fiscal straits were his invention. She still trusted his honesty, if she didn't trust his character.

There was a lull. As in the Second World War, it took some time to get from the declarations to the battlefields. Julius had not yet found his dream house; not established even what his dream house was. He would, in fact, be two years searching.

Evelyn spent these two years in dread of what she felt was now inevitable. Every spare moment and weekend that she had, Julius dragged her away househunting. At first they looked at cottages, but it was soon discovered that solid farmhouses could be had for not much more. The farmhouses they went to see – and the vicarages – became increasingly grand until they were looking at courts and manors and halls and houses on the slippery principle that the larger the house, the greater its value, and that it did no harm to look.

BY THE END of Julius's search, Evelyn's mind had begun to be at ease. It seemed that his fixation with the country would come to nothing. She felt sure that no house in England could ever match Julius's ideals, and so she indulged his searching as a strange hobby. It became pleasant to spend spare time looking at other people's houses. Indeed, she wrote a successful television play about a ghostly couple who could never find a house to which they belonged. Her novels were being made into films, and her television series were being made into novels. Julius seemed to spend his entire time searching for the house, but she only had time to look over the shortlists. He would pick her up from her script meetings or from the airport, and they would go to see the Georgian gems and the Jacobean magnificences. Usually, Julius was seeing the place for the second time when they saw it together, and, in his reviewing, would find some irreconcilable fault in the house or the gardens or the surrounding countryside. Evelyn could only agree with his opinion, and they would retreat to the next issue of *Country Life*.

For this hiatus of two years, Julius and Evelyn almost developed a friendship, or a fondness for one another. They were each completely wrapped in their own concerns, and only met on neutral and uncontroversial territory. Benedict and Hannah were at their universities. Life in Hampstead resolved itself into a sub-platonic *laissez-aller*. Because there was barely any need to communicate, there was barely any need to disagree. Each could imagine at this time that they were compatible with the other.

And so, on this plane, in this frame of mind, they came to the end of the second winter. A house called Ryme came to their attention. Unusually, they both saw it for the first time together. It was in Somerset, ten miles south of the Bennets. It was a vast house with several cottages. The details said that there were seventeen acres of garden and ten of arboretum and thirty of farmland.

The first sight they had of this place was an extraordinary thing. They came through that landscape of small hills between Bruton and Shepton Mallet, that is like a Chinese representation of landscape in its form, and saw it within the privacy of this rucking and folding country, on a clinging, foggy day in late February, when the air was heavy and white, and the dark masses of the trees and hedges stood out in relief against the opaque atmosphere. All noise was drowned by the solidity of the mist, and the mist itself was cut through with the cold, which made the atmosphere light rather than oppressive.

They came in view of the house which, in this air, gave the impression that it floated, like a ship on a pond. The first moment they saw it there was a red deer hind gazing at them from the lawns, which vanished with their coming. The house remained, veined with the stems of ancient roses, crowned in castellations and figured with window tracery.

Evelyn's heart sank. She knew that the suspension of her sentence of exile was over. She knew that Julius would buy this house, that this house was the mythical countryside in which his belief had persisted. If there was a doubt, it was that she wondered whether this house was to be Elba or St Helena to her.

The house was an exquisite lure to Julius. Neither the buildings nor the gardens felt as though they existed in modern England, and were as though they had nothing to do with the suburban Somerset all about them. By microclimate, by microlandscape, they were cut off from everything. They had nothing to do with reality or with mental progression. It was a place for lotus-eating, for existing in a self-indulgent vacuum. All this was apparent both to Evelyn and to Julius in that first sighting which left her paralysed with horror and dread, and made him immovable with ecstasy.

With what time and energy she had, Evelyn fought against Ryme and against Julius's determination. But you might as well have taken a shovel against a mountain. Only faith would persuade you that the mountain had moved.

Evelyn had no faith. Her independence had stolen upon her without her asking for it. Once it had come, she had worked and overworked to maintain what she was and increase what she was, but still felt that she had no security of tenure: that her profession had been lent to her, and that it could be recalled. Her success as a feminist had been due, in part, to the limited nature of her liberation. When she wrote about the tyranny of men and the lives of women, she wasn't theorising, but explaining a process in which she was a current participant. Of which she was victim.

Ryme became central to their lives. The house in Frognal was put on the market and sold. Of course, no penny of it went towards Evelyn's debts or her taxes. Julius carried it all off with his usual flair for confusing figures. If Julius owed you money, and you went to claim it from him, he would always convince you that it was you who owed him money. If you were silly enough to owe him money, you usually found that you had to pay it at least twice over. And his logic was always a sound structure.

So Julius bought Ryme for himself. If Evelyn wanted a roof over her head, she had to go and live there with him. There was nowhere else for her to go (I offered her a room in our house, but she only told me that I was awfully sweet). At that moment, she was utterly broke; hounded by Mr Blomfield and without even a lover to fall back on. No matter what she did, Ryme would have her. By June, she was completely cut off from London.

Julius produced a legal document, which he said she must sign, by which she renounced any claim on his property. He said it was a usual formality which the bank insisted on before giving him a mortgage. What he did not tell her was that he was applying for a token mortgage of a thousand pounds, simply so that she should have to sign this agreement. Evelyn still had no idea that Julius was rich; that he had paid the greater part of the purchase price of Ryme by selling five paintings from his collection.

Evelyn signed his document. At the time it seemed a minor insult among all the injury she was subject to. She tried, for her own sake, to settle into Ryme as quickly as possible. She colonised one of the smaller sitting-rooms and made it her office. Julius had the rest of the house more or less to himself. For weeks he simply scuttled from room to room, accumulating importance as he went, and planning ways to spread himself over as much space as possible.

It soon became apparent to Evelyn that Julius was working against the house. He installed computers in the drawing-room and converted it into his office. The fact that he seemed to have no work to do only compounded this injury. Neither did he confine his misuse to the house. Soon after they moved, he announced that he was going to just tidy up the arboretum, and proceeded to go through it with a chainsaw, this man who wouldn't know a holly from an ivy. Someone once told him that a conifer was an ugly thing, and so, by the end of July, five mature specimen junipers had been removed from the gardens.

Perversely enough, it was these acts of vandalism which gave Evelyn her first sympathy for Ryme. One can't sit in an office and bristle for ever. She watched Julius's pillaging until it occurred to her that, unless she stepped in to counterbalance and deflect him, the entire place would be ruined.

In the event, it was Ryme that survived and her career that was ruined. Evelyn neglected her novels and became a chatelaine. The maintenance of the house, and particularly the garden, seduced her away from her reality. Despite the pressures of her agent, her publisher and her public, she never wrote another word from the time that she moved to Ryme. Once, for an outstanding commitment, she booked herself into a large, anonymous hotel in London for a month, and wrote a book of short stories. But the revenue from it hardly paid the hotel bill, and when she came back to Ryme there was so much to do that she could never bear to leave it again.

As for Julius's literary career: once his initial burst of zeal had been used in wrecking the house, he left everything to Evelyn, and did nothing more than read the paper every morning. He told himself (and me), through this lassitude, that he was resting and plotting but, really, he had come as far in his ambitions as his abilities could take him. Poor Julius, the fading flower. He was to have just one more attempt at youth and brilliance. But we can give him up from here on. He became less and less interesting. He achieved nothing more in his life, except the complete alienation of all his country neighbours who, although they were perfectly friendly at first, soon became incensed with his complete ignorance and his arrogant refusals of help or advice.

And me. Sometimes I drove down to Ryme Episcopi on fine days, and just sat in my car on a part of the road from which I could see the gardens, waiting for a glimpse of Evelyn. There were times when I felt that she had betrayed me after she left London. I think that she sensed this and, when she came up for more than a day, she stayed with Sarah Bliss rather than with us. What could I do?

I HAVE SOMETIMES asked myself whether Hugh Longford is a fictional character. Whether I have invented him and he is only a phantom of my longing for Evelyn. For I never felt any jealousy over Hugh Longford. I never wished him ill. It could be that this was because he was the first man to make Evelyn happy. I believe that he was the first man she loved. She should have loved me, but now that was neither here nor there. I had almost given up wishing for my own happiness. When Hugh turned up I could see the possibility of Evelyn's happiness, and, after all, that had always been half of my ambition.

There was something, too, in Hugh Longford that reminded me of my own self at his age. I cannot say what it is. His looks have nothing in common with mine. His mind is a vastly different thing. The only tangible thing that we have in common is our love for Evelyn. When you have been the sole incumbent of a passion like this for twenty years, it is nice to meet a fellow sufferer. I am as fond of Hugh Longford as I have been of any man.

One autumn, in the middle of these Eighties, when Evelyn Cotton had spent her second summer at Ryme, Hugh Longford came to Somerset. He had a face that was dished like that of an Arab horse, and there was something mournful about him. He had just been through the tiresome process of losing his faith and love and youth and innocence. He was a thatcher who, until this moment, had plied his trade at the wilder end of Country Wexford.

It had been said that the wildness at that end of Wexford was due, in part, to him. Whether it was or not, he had the worst reputation of all the Forth and Bargy men.

It is not through Hugh himself that I know his reputation or his reasons for leaving Wexford. He is not someone to talk about the past. He only seems aware of the present. I do not think that he imagines that I know as much about him as I do; but I had heard his legend a long time before I met him.

I had been a few times to the Wexford Festival, and had heard him talked about by men who had daughters. From what I heard, I expected an extraordinary, manic seducer who was permanently inebriated and charming with it. From things he has said, but more from knowing him, and from things I heard in Ireland and from things his sister has said, I think I have pieced him together as well as anyone could.

The Forth and Bargy trappings, and to some extent his trade, were all an affectation to him. At sixteen he had eschewed the cosy intellectual background supplied by his parents, and apprenticed himself to an old thatcher. It had all to do with the romance of manual labour and rural crafts. By thatching he had supported himself and a hard-drinking, unrestrained lifestyle until his mid-twenties. His amorous reputation, and the vast numbers of girls who had been willing to be part of it, were legend. Perhaps it was only legend for, through all of it, none of them was ever known to take the boat for him. He had self-possession and charm in greater abundance than many of us have encountered. Some would have called him arrogant, but not many.

In the spring of 1984, he had the misfortune to think himself in love. She was a sharp little *hausfrau* of the kind that is generally best avoided. You have no great need to know the details. She betrayed him. She broke his shining heart, the existence of which had been doubted. She ground the last ounce of despair out of him, once and for all. She humiliated him before himself. She increased her own importance by making a conquest of him, and by spurning him, once she had done so. She degraded him. She forced him to take life seriously. She made him grow up.

He left Ireland to be allowed to grow up in peace: to escape from his own legend and be allowed to behave as he wished, as his new, more sober self would want to behave, without the expectations of all the people who used to spend so much of their time cheering him on or disapproving of him.

A small patching job of two weeks' duration brought him to Somerset. It was the house of some friends of his parents, who lived quietly in Ryme Episcopi. He stayed with them the first two weeks of October, disliking the England that he saw, and intending to move on to Normandy as soon as he could arrange some work there.

England, what could he see in it? The villages were overcrowded and the fields between them too enormous. There seemed to be nothing natural or old about it. There were ancient houses, but they were all double-glazed and overpointed and restored to within inches of newness. Every barn that might have once been nice had a family of burgeoning stockbrokers living within its converted walls. What wasn't frozen by the preservers was destroyed by the developers. He could see nothing in the English that made him want to thatch their houses.

On the twelfth of October, he was offered some work on a house called Ryme. He thought, as nothing else was in the offing, he might as well go and look at it.

You may think that the rest is inevitable. You may think he only has to stride in, and Evelyn will be swept into his arms, and there is nothing more to be said. But nothing is ever as simple as that. This, after all, is a tragedy and not a romance. And you wonder, in any case, if there is such a thing as love.

To begin with, it was Julius he dealt with. It was Julius who had decided to have the Long Barn rethatched. To begin with, it was Ryme that kept Hugh Longford in England. To begin with, Evelyn was nowhere to be seen.

Hugh Longford did not take the instant dislike to Julius that I might have expected. There is no reason for this that I can give you. Perhaps Hugh never gave Julius enough thought to dislike him. Perhaps it is that I have painted too black a picture of my villain. He was no Quilp, after all. He never strangled any babies that I have heard of. He did have friends of his own who found him to be amusing and intelligent company. Don't think by this that I have misjudged Julius. But it is just possible that if you were a tolerant sort of person and only had a slight acquaintance with him, you might see no reason to dislike him particularly. I have seen the worst of him, again and again.

68

However you or I may feel about Julius, Hugh Longford had no strong feeling either way. He treated Julius with the deference and indifference due to a client. He telephoned the Camargue for the reeds he needed, and by the fourteenth of October he had moved into the South Cottage.

Hugh Longford was entranced with Ryme. He found in it the inversion of everything that repelled him about the England beyond. He felt himself cut off from coy urbanisation of the countryside. He thought that he could spend some time here.

The South Cottage was a miniature. It was barely big enough for one person, but that was perfect for Hugh. It was at the end of the arboretum, surrounded by the oak collection. He could count *Quercus cerris, Quercus rubra, Quercus coccinea, Quercus ilex* and then stop, cursing the limits of his knowledge that prevented him from separating and knowing the other seventy-one species of oak in his neck of the woods.

From his upstairs window, he could see across and through the trees to a paddock of steps in the hillside. Lippizaners, of the Conversano line, recently given into Evelyn's care, grazed skittishly on these terraces in good weather. Between the trees, from his front doorstep, there was a prospect that led to the sculpted yew hedges on the lawns, and beyond, to the window where Evelyn sometimes sat at her idle desk.

Moving to Ryme, Hugh Longford, for the first time since his childhood, felt something akin to the confident state of happiness that is to do with wellbeing, to do with the premonition that there is goodness to come: a feeling that one is looked after, and that basic optimism is justifiable.

That bright mild October, Hugh put his ladders to the Long Barn, and began to remove the old reed from the roof. And it was from the roof that he could see into every part of the gardens and every room at the back of the house. Framed in one window, the first day, there was a woman of indeterminate age whom he took to be the wife of Julius Drake. She came and went past the window, and her walk was remarkable because she held her body rigid and behind the vertical, and because she glided as though she had no feet and was being pulled about on a trolley.

She came and went in the window, but the impression he retained of her was indistinct. Her hair was brown with henna and

69

shone like furniture. The colour of her eyes was hidden in the angle of her face but, occasionally, he caught a glimpse of piercing yellow.

In the days that followed he would see her in the house but, more usually, about the gardens, setting the borders straight for winter. He began to be aware of a compulsion he had to speak to her, but he fought shy of seeking her out. He stayed on his roof and followed her from between his reed bundles, as Evelyn in pink acetate stooped among the green lawns and the dark hedges and the soft lichens on the stones.

One Sunday morning he woke late in his cottage, but thought from the way that the light was coming in the window that it might be the beginning of spring. You know those autumn days you could swear at the time were fresher than spring. It was a blinding light that washed out the limewashed room for the ten minutes it took him to open his eyes, a searing light that disappeared the moment he set foot out of bed. He went out in the wood and the clean-coloured morning, not doubting the wonders that might be in it, and he saw Evelyn on the hill with her horses, all staggered on the slope.

There were three of them, all boys and all nuzzling her in the breast and pushing her in the back and raking the ground up with their feet, demanding a turn at the bucket.

Her hair had a shine that day you would think had been put in with an airbrush. She wore a skirt of shot pink silk and her cardigan had pearls sewn into the grey cashmere. Clothes from the days of the Harrods account, which she wore now as a sort of defiance against the supremacy of her new life. Her Wellington boots were a size too large for her, and you could see by the way she stood that she was cold.

Hugh stood in the boundary and saw every detail. Is it necessary to tell you the rest? To describe to you the curve of her waist, or the shape of her backside? Would that sort of voyeurism mean anything to you? Think, instead, of your own ideal of a backside and a waist, and insert it here. I hate audience participation, don't you?

Hugh passed beneath and around the bottom of the hill to come upon the road for Ryme Episcopi, while she, unaware of him, was jostled up the hill by her horses. When her bucket was empty, she left it on the ground and walked to the ridge to see where the white cyclamen grew beneath the hazel trees and to see down the valley, beyond the east windbreak of hawthorn, and to look back at the house, just to stand on top of the ridge and watch her horses from another angle.

Looking down the road towards the pub in the village, she saw a figure going along, with more of a stride than a walk, and a long coat swinging out behind him. After her came the noise of the horses kicking their rubber bucket down the hill, and before her was the man she was avoiding; though if you asked her whether she was avoiding him she would deny it, and if you asked her why she was avoiding him, she couldn't tell you. She knew that something was going to happen, and for it all to be right, she had to stand still and watch it happen around her.

She wasn't afraid of Hugh Longford, but she was wary of her fascination with him, and she couldn't see that she had any freedom to pursue her curiosity, if that is what it was. She watched him out of sight, as though he were one of her horses. As though, in time, he would come to her.

It was that Sunday that Julius and Evelyn threw a great luncheon party for all the Bennets, and Paul and Vera Boldt, and the Drummers and the Canters, and poor Elspeth Freeman, who was newly abandoned and in need of comfort. David and Emir Magna came in another contingent with Sarah Bliss. These were all their present friends, and, apart from Sarah, constituted the society which Somerset afforded them. Older, deeper friends could come down from London but, as far as society goes, proximity is the main thing.

Sally and I had been asked, and we had meant to come, but we were frying other fish that Sunday. Perhaps I loved Sally. Perhaps I never did; but, either way, it is hard not to be upset when a marriage falls away from you. Perhaps the version of my marriage with Sally that I have given you has been coloured by recent events. Perhaps I would have told you something else the day before yesterday. I have a sudden horror, a guilt, that I have been dismissive about my own children, about the mother of my children. I have said that they were all nothing to me. Were they really nothing to me? Or am I blinded by my obsession? Although I meant to insinuate myself as little as possible, I have come to a part

71

of this story which I begin to realise has scarred me. There is still a pain in my amputated leg. But you can't want to know about me, or my crumbling marriage that never really was. You want to be at luncheon with Evelyn Cotton. I can describe the scene to you better than if I had been there. The only things I can really remember are the things which come to me second-hand: scenes I have never witnessed, but which have been described to me later.

By all accounts, especially the most glowing, this party was gruesome. Most of the people were of the same sort as the Bennets: painters and writers and left-wing ruralists. The odd self-satisfied architect. David and Emir Magna did not quite belong. David Magna was a small, vain and silent man. Nobody had a good opinion of him because nobody had ever heard an opinion from him. Emir, his wife, was large and voluble and vulnerable. She was popular in her own right, but was isolated by her self-effacement and the unpopularity of the man attached to her. Her best friend was Sarah Bliss, and the polarity of their existences seemed to be only conducive to their friendship.

Sarah Bliss was quite extraordinary because of the un-compromising level at which she lived her life and her ability to be independent of her men, dispensing with them once they had become redundant.

She looked a lot like Evelyn Cotton, in certain lights, and the first time I met her, I went rushing up to her thinking that it was Evelyn. When I introduced her to Evelyn, they became instant friends, as though they had a natural link between them, like identical twins. I sometimes wondered if Sarah had replaced me as Evelyn's chief confidant, but I don't think that their friendship was a verbal one. At the time of this party, Sarah was in the process of shedding her man. None of us knew about this until long afterwards. At the time the only signs were that she hardly spoke and wouldn't listen. She looked out of the window and took no notice of what was going on in the room.

That terrible party. We have an interest, the reason for which will become clear later, in Paul and Vera Boldt. He was a potter, and a lumbering man of no refinement, physical or mental. She was a flimsy basket-maker and semi-professional conquestador. In her time, she had made off with almost every man in that room. Julius Drake was the exception. Being a thorough woman – a fact you could observe if you had watched her working the party, rolling her eyes and being vivacious for everyone in turn – she was not far off remedying her omission. She had already won the affections of Julius, and was close to claiming his body.

Unaware of this propensity in Vera Boldt, Evelyn had been accepting bosom friendship from her all of that summer. They had swopped clothing and gynaecological confidences and been happy to be often in each other's company, without any suspicion, on Evelyn's part, of what was to come.

By the time of this party, the situation had gone beyond retrieve. Although the affair had not yet been consummated, it was a known fact to most of the first contingent, and was beginning to be suspected by Evelyn. That afternoon she watched them closely, while trying to behave normally. It was hard not to see that they were behaving oddly, almost farcically: pointedly avoiding each other as they moved about the room, and nodding discreetly and glancing meaningfully, and coming together suddenly in a whispering huddle every so often. Then Julius came up to Evelyn rather abruptly and said he had just better go and check on the sheep, and shot out of the room by way of the french windows. Exactly fifteen minutes later, Vera sidled up to Evelyn and said she was so sorry but she must be leaving, she had to go and see her mother, but Paul would stay and come home with the Bennets. She then kissed all her friends in a hurry, tipping winks to some of them, and made a dash for the door.

Evelyn, numbed by this meat on the bones of her suspicion, was unsure of how to act, react or dissemble. She felt sure that she wasn't going to follow them, or descend to their level of melodrama by showing that she had noticed anything. She could hardly bear the idea of following them and being made to look foolish by the fact that they might be doing nothing as she came upon them. So she stayed where she was and attended to her party, and waited for the time to think about it all.

Meanwhile, Hugh Longford was putting in an hour of the afternoon on the roof of the barn. He knew that there must be a party from the number of cars that were parked beneath the barn. He was interested to observe that he felt no resentment at being excluded from the party. Six months before and he would have felt obliged to attend, invited or not. Now he was happier not to meet new people or have the strain of being amusing put upon him. He had grown out of the age of compulsive revelry.

From the ridge of the roof, he saw Julius appear in the car park and pace up and down, his wristwatch held before him, and an expression of extraordinary anxiety on his face. Hugh was about to call out and bid him the time of day, when a women darted out from the house.

She was a markedly thin, agile woman of quick, definite movement. She had a peculiar way of holding her eyes wide open, as though she were trying to give the impression that they were enormous. Her yellow bleached hair sliced the air with each jerking movement of her head. As soon as he saw her, Julius slid into the passenger seat of one of the cars. She halted, and then began to move towards this car in a bizarre manner, glancing about her like a secret agent, and sliding from pillar to post. With one last furtive scan of the house, she joined Julius in the car where, having risked a single rapturous kiss, they sat in earnest conversation, holding hands tightly across the handbrake.

Hugh drew his head below the roofline, feeling that it would be better if they failed to notice him. Unable to make complete sense of what he saw, he concentrated on his work and waited for things to become clearer.

That evening, Julius decided to visit Hugh in the South Cottage. Hugh was embarrassed at first, not being sure whether he had been seen on the roof that afternoon, but Julius was all ease and affability, seeming terribly pleased with himself and the world about him. Hugh thought for a moment that he was about to be confided in, but the moment, to his relief, passed.

Julius hung on, although he seemed to have nothing to talk about. He stood, on one leg and then the other, at the same time quite puffed out in the chest, as though the upper half of his anatomy was boasting and the lower half was unsure. Hugh began to wish he would leave, but offered him coffee.

Julius refused copiously and said that he found coffee over-stimulating. He leered as he said the last word, and then fell silent, gazing straight at Hugh in expectation. Hugh could think of no response. He knew that he was supposed to guffaw knowingly, but found the whole situation too peculiar. He turned his back and looked out the window.

'Do you have an interest in horses?' he asked, nodding toward the Lippizaners.

Julius replied with a hurt abruptness, 'You will have to ask Evelyn about the horses. They are nothing to do with me.'

Julius was disappointed as he left the cottage. He had gone in with the idea that he and Hugh could be soulmates. That Hugh, being as young, in fact, as Julius felt these days, would understand his elation instantly. That he would exclaim, 'Ah! I can see that you are in love. Who is the lucky girl? Come to the pub and tell me all about it, you dog!' That they would talk of love and life and art, and became intoxicated with their common free spirit. That it would be impossible for Hugh not to become infected with the enthusiasm that glowed from Julius's every feature.

In his disappointment, the only self-saving conclusion that Julius could come to was that Hugh was as arrogant as he seemed. Hugh, floored in the wake of Julius's invasion, decided that Julius was slightly mad.

Perhaps Julius was by this time slightly mad. He was certainly male-menopausal and behaving in a fashion which may have been appealing in a teenager, but was grotesque in someone of his age and station. It is possible that love makes one mad, and equally possible that one has to be mad to fall in love. We do not grudge Julius his falling in love. You cannot be too old or too villainous to fall in love, but you can be old enough to know how to behave yourself.

Julius returned to a bad-tempered Evelyn, by this time in a bad temper himself, and they spent a not unusual evening snarling at each other from opposite ends of the house.

EVELYN COTTON AND Hugh Longford had to meet at some point, no matter how much their instincts drew them back from the meeting. From his roof Hugh had an almost constant view of Evelyn and knew in detail how she spent her day. She, from the desk of her office, had several views of him: the back of his head on the roof; his profile as he bashed the bundles of reed against the brick floor of the yard; the swinging length of him as he short-cut across the lawns to and from the South Cottage. She saw these angles and bided her time. It was her nature to watch things from a distance, to note them and record them. She was never drawn to anything or anyone, but found that they were drawn to her. Besides all which, she felt that this was not a good time to risk compromising herself. She wanted to keep a moral advantage over Julius in the battle that was to come.

Eventually, they spoke to each other. Hugh began the conversation, partly because he had stored so many questions from his rooftop observations, partly because at the time she was committing an act which he couldn't bear to witness.

He was on his roof as usual, and she had led a horse into the yard and tied it up for grooming. She was working quietly as though she was unaware of his presence. Hugh watched her, and realised for the first time since he had left Ireland that he was lonely. He watched her and the horse and envied the companionship that was between them. He thought that he might get a dog or a cat, because you could never love an animal enough to break

76

your heart. He thought he might call down to her and ask if it was all right for him to keep a dog in the South Cottage, when he realised that it wasn't a dog he wanted at all, only the excuse to call down to her.

While half of his mind was dwelling on his need for a shred of human contact, the other half was criticising her method of grooming the horse. When she came to the tail, he could stand it no longer.

'Stop!' he yelled in a sort of pleading voice that was embarrassing to him as soon as he had said it. She brushed on as though she hadn't heard him, or if she had, she couldn't see that the exhortation had anything to do with herself. In the moments that it took her to stop her brushing and look up towards him, he wondered if it wouldn't be better to go on with his thatching and pretend that he had said nothing.

She looked at him over the rump of the horse, and he saw that he had no choice but to continue. He thought that he would sound most convincing if there was a note of irritation in his voice.

'How could you take that class of a brush to a horse's tail?' He spoke to her as if he was a guardian angel, nudging her back into the path of righteousness. He spoke as if his soul was grieved with her action.

She looked at him as if she doubted his presence, and then she looked at the brush, and then she breathed a sigh of tried patience, and she said, 'Well, what am I supposed to do?'

'Tease it out, hair by hair,' he said as he descended his ladders, his kneepads clapping against his knees. She had a moment's thought that he looked like one of the angels, descending to instruct her. She suppressed this as he reached the end of the ladder and turned towards her, so that her face was back to a mask of dignified disbelief.

'I've never done anything to my horses' tails,' he continued, 'except wash them before and after hunting. If you want a thick tail, you must never brush it.'

'But they get knotted,' she said.

'Then pull it apart, hair by hair.' He began to show her how to do it. She watched him, noncommittally, and they continued in silence for five minutes until she said, not expecting him to know what a Lippizaner was, 'They are Lippizaners, you know.'

'One of them is. The other two are crosses,' he said.

She was seriously offended by what she saw as a denunciation. He had succeeded in knocking her off her perch. When she asked him how he knew, or what made him think it, her voice had lost the tone of artificial banter.

'They are too light. Probably they have been crossed with Arabs, or Andalucians if you are lucky. Did you buy them as Lippizaners?'

'They aren't mine,' she admitted. The air between them became full and heavy, as though they were a couple already, and could fall out with each other; as though a relationship had been established between them before they had met. Evelyn became aware of this intimacy, into which they had fallen without exchanging a single serious phrase. She hauled herself back on to her perch.

'You seem to know a lot about horses,' she said.

'Only the tail,' he said. He tried to make a joke of it; to turn on her with the full blast of his charm; to give an impression of rows of white teeth and a hero of romance. But she was looking down at him from her perch. He would have to go further and, somehow, apologise for his cruelty. 'It's a bit embarrassing really,' he said. 'I had a friend who worked at the Spanish School.'

He had fawned at her feet and been forgiven. She drew herself back from haughtiness and into a condition of stately amusement, and, with an erotic turn to her mouth, she said that she could think of much more embarrassing things than that.

Her remark made him feel sheepish. He thought that she was bringing her age and experience and station and Englishness to bear in order to suppress him. She was feeling equally sheepish, but at her age had learnt to disguise it better. She had believed in the purity of her horses and the Conversano line; she had, if anything, embroidered the fiction which the vulgar woman who owned them had given her.

She says that it was at this moment that she knew she had met her equal in Hugh Longford.

They talked. I have had accounts from both of them of this first conversation. It is hard to know what was said then and what was said later. The intimacy which they claimed to have from the beginning seems incredible to me; seems more like indiscretion. He stood behind the horse, working his way through the tail, and asking her questions about the house and what she and Julius did

78

for a living. These questions had been eating at him, since they plainly weren't farmers or gentry, or any of the other kinds of people who occupied large houses in his experience.

'Julius,' she said, 'is an accountant. I am a writer.'

'Serious or pulp?'

'Novels,' she said.

He straightened up. 'Ah no, you're not serious.'

'Say that again,' she said.

'What?'

'It's just that you sounded particularly Irish.'

He ignored this, and asked her if she was famous.

'I think so,' she said. 'They have just translated me into French for the first time. That is rather a compliment. The French are so xenophobic and occupied with their own literature that it tends to be the last language you get translated into. A sort of final accolade.'

'Are your books funny,' he asked, 'or sad?'

'It depends which language you read them in. The Norwegians always greet me with gales of laughter, while the Swedes are always terribly sympathetic, and are under the impression that my life must be tragic.'

'It sounds as though I should have heard of you,' he said. 'What name do you write under?'

'My own,' she answered, evasively. For a reason which she was unable to analyse at that moment, she didn't want him to identify her with her books. She didn't know whether she was ashamed of her books or ashamed of herself. Finally, she thought that it would be coy to withhold her name, and so she said it.

'Evelyn what?' he said.

'Cotton,' she repeated, 'as in "Summertime".'

'I suppose,' he said, 'that I don't have a great grasp of modern literature.'

'It is nice to think that you don't know everything about everything.'

He finished the tail, and his excuse for talking to her, and they stood in silence for a moment, looking at it, and then she said, as if to put him at his ease, but also to defend herself, 'I have a son who is about your age.'

'I am not as young as I look,' he said, feeling that she had dismissed him by what she said. He looked at her closely, and saw now that, although she looked young, her age was no longer indeterminable. He saw that she was another generation from him, as they say, old enough to be his mother. She was another species. He felt at ease then. There was no longer a possibility of love in it. This was no one you could break your heart over after all.

'My son was named after an Irish poet,' she said.

'Who?' he asked.

'Someone his father knew, at Oxford. His father was of Irish stock.'

'What was he called? I might know them,' he said.

'I don't think you would,' she said. 'They were working class and lived in Bradford.'

'Ireland is a classless society,' he said. 'But I never thought so until I came to England.'

'Julius wanted us to move to Ireland, before we came here.'

'He wouldn't have liked it,' said Hugh. 'I can't think that he likes it here. You seem to like it here.'

'I didn't want to come,' she said. 'Julius had to drag me here, kicking and screaming. I couldn't imagine living anywhere except London.'

He said that London was the only place he couldn't imagine living in.

'You would like it if you were there,' she said.

'I would die,' he said.

Afterwards, she thought of this as a sort of prophecy. A warning that she should have heeded. She said that the first days she knew Hugh Longford were crammed with portents and signs. That she was hedged in by the inevitability of everything. In the circumstances, there was nothing they could do but to try to forget the atmosphere of heavy premonition and form an easy friendship. They saw each other daily and, before long, she felt sure enough of him to lend him one of her books to read. It took her a week to decide which one she would give him. She was nervous of uncovering herself; she thought that, if he had any idea of how she really was, their friendship would be blown. Perhaps that is why she gave him her most inscrutable book.

She gave him *The Sisters of Mercy*. Do you know it? It is perhaps the best, and the least read, Evelyn Cotton novel; a massive, rambling book of seventy pages that the *Guardian* had hailed as the 'Feminist *Ulysses*'. Once you begin to read it, there is no way back out again. I have never been able to re-read it, because my first impression was so perfect. I can remember feeling that I had grown ten years in wisdom after I had put it down and, at the same time, the plot is so simple. A small girl and her grandmother, that is all, simply and sparingly drawn.

Hugh Longford brought the small book back to the South Cottage with him, and skirted around it for a day or two, as though it was a cyanide capsule and he hadn't yet decided to die. He could sense that to read the book would be to start an irreversible process. He finally picked it up one evening in preference to the inanity of the television.

Early the next morning, as Evelyn crossed the yard with her log basket, she was stopped by another shout from the Long Barn. She turned and saw Hugh Longford leaping through a window like a circus dog.

'I read it,' he was shouting. He was waving her book around. His eyes were bleary but his expression was animated.

'What do you think?' she asked.

The question stopped him; floored him. How could he have said what he thought? He had been up all night thinking. He had never thought so much in his life. How could he begin to express all of that in a sentence of speech?

He said it was remarkable. He repeated the word remarkable four times.

She plastered her face in smiles. She felt it was the first time she had had a compliment or a favourable review. She had that feeling, which not many of us are privileged to experience, that she had done some good by what she had written. That she was not a waste of this planet's space and oxygen.

'What are you writing now?' he said.

She was caught out. She knew that there must have been a good reason for not giving him the book. If he hadn't liked the book, he would have thought little of her for having written it. As he had liked the book, he would think little of her because she had stopped writing.

'I haven't written anything for a while,' she said. She prepared herself for criticism. She was ready to be told off for idleness, for wasting her talent and her time, and for being a disappointment to the world.

'I suppose,' he said, 'if you have written this, there isn't much else to be said.'

She told me afterwards that he had absolved all of her guilt for not writing with this one sentence. He had explained why her pencil didn't move when she put it on the paper. Why it was more important to be dividing Japanese anemones. She had nothing more to say, for the moment.

IT WAS ABOUT this time, November or so, that Benedict came down from Bath for a weekend and met Hugh Longford.

By this time, Benedict Cotton was about twenty-two. He was tall and athletic and the image of his mother or, to be more accurate, of his late maternal grandfather. He had his mother's brand of amorphous innocence about him, combined with his father's irrational temperament. His face had a tendency to look sulky which, at his age, was not unattractive. He had a way of concealing his wit, and of laughing at us all in secret. This was a characteristic which I admired. I took it to denote self-sufficiency, and a healthy mistrust of mankind. He was reading architecture at Bath. It was a subject in which his only interest was ideological and for which he had little aptitude. His tutors said that there was a great future for him in the profession, but then Bath was an old-fashioned school where modernism still prevailed.

Benedict took to the thatching immediately, and for the entire weekend his silhouette perched itself on the ridge, close to Hugh's. He was not much help in any practical sense, but a pleasant companion to have at that altitude. Hugh told me afterwards that, although he liked Benedict, he was wary of him, for some reason unknown to him at the time. The reason seemed so obvious to me. I, who have dealt with and known the Cottons for so many years.

You fall in love with someone and you think that everything about her is wonderful and unique to her. You are amazed by the beauty of her every small gesture, and in your love you isolate everything that you take to be an individual trait of hers. These are your treasures. The things you can recall to make yourself happy or miserable from time to time.

Then, one by one, or perhaps by the roomful, you will meet her family. There may be no obvious physical resemblances within the family, but at sometime there will be an expression of the mouth or a turn of phrase that you recognise. For a moment, your pupils dilate and you feel a twinge of emotion which you previously thought could only be triggered by the person that you love. You stop yourself, so embarrassed, that later you will deny it to yourself. I have felt this with Benedict and with Evelyn's mother and with her brother. I have felt it with Sarah Bliss, who is no relation of Evelyn, but is so like her. You realise that the person you love is not unique in every detail, but only a unique mixture of common details. And you still love these details because, in all probability, these details were what you loved first. And so, I can see Hugh Longford, who at this stage was still unaware of the way in which he loved Evelyn, sitting on the ridge of the Long Barn with Benedict, and seeing a twist of the mouth or a turn of the fingers, and feeling for a moment the twinge of attraction without knowing why, and suppressing it immediately for his own sake, but becoming wary of Benedict.

Perhaps I am wrong. Perhaps it was too soon for Hugh to be in love with Evelyn (except that we are always in love for a long time before we realise it), and all he felt was a premonition of the anger which Benedict was later to show him. And I must be wrong, because I have taken this many words to describe one tiny sliver of the atmosphere at Ryme that weekend. I thought it was important because it is so hard to know what men (including myself) really feel about anything. We are so busy trying to be straightforward that I wonder if we feel anything at all.

They worked on the roof. Because of the microclimate of Ryme, it never rained in the daytime, and so work could be done all the daylight hours that were given. This good weather seemed bizarre and at the same time natural to a place such as Ryme. Benedict talked, easily and freely. He only needed the encouragement of the odd intelligent interjection from Hugh; the odd sign that Hugh was at all interested in what he had to say. By the time that he went back to Bath they had become friends.

The Monday brought silence to Hugh Longford on the roof. He was as pleased by the novelty of the quietness as he had been by the novelty of the talking. And now I think he must have been in love with Evelyn Cotton, because he stood on his ladders and thought that he would like to stay at Ryme. He felt there was something holding him there. At the time he thought it was the place itself. He wondered if it would be possible for him to rent the South Cottage from Julius after he had finished the Long Barn, and use Ryme as a base for his business. But other events overtook him.

About the end of November, Evelyn decided that she had had her fill of Julius. She should have been used to him having affairs. In the past she had always stood by and never gone in for exposure and drama. But this time, Julius was playing the mooning lovesick adolescent more than usual, and the society in which they were moving was so small that the affair was known to everyone around her. She was tired of people tactfully keeping things from her, sick of Vera Boldt's fawning friendship and glutted with her own suspicions. She couldn't see that she had anything to lose by making a fuss about the affair. She thought that a fuss was due to her. Perhaps she was bored. Perhaps she thought that Vera Boldt was a real threat. Afterwards she always said that Vera Boldt's only reason for seducing an old bag of bones like Julius was to get her hands on Ryme. Vera was jealous of Evelyn's station in life. Well, we all knew that.

On top of all of this, her agent was on the phone to her every other day about an anthology of women's writing which, in a moment of weakness, she had agreed to edit. And she needed the money. In spite of earning practically nothing but royalties since she had moved to Ryme, she still had the children's education to pay for and her mother to support and the household at Ryme to provide for. If it had been left to Julius to buy food they would have been gnawing old roots from the garden. Her bank manager had removed all of the plastic, and had refused payment on some of her cheques. She had nothing left to live on but the Harrods account.

She decided to go to London and meet people and make arrangements and see if she couldn't get some work for herself. She spent days on the phone, setting it all up. The world seemed pleased at the prospect of having her back. When the morning came for her to catch her train, Julius was all dancing attendance and seemed eager to drive her to the station. As he normally couldn't care less and would leave her to get a taxi rather than waste his petrol, she became suspicious of his behaviour. To see how he would react, she announced that she had changed her mind and would not go to London that day. She watched the colour drain from his face and the panic rise through his features. He began to persuade her to change her mind, but found that he was making things worse with his incoherence. He found it impossible to disguise his consternation and disappointment. He drew in his breath to calm himself, barked something at her about his having work to do, and then he set off at a diarrhoeic run for his study.

Evelyn knew for certain then. She realised that it wasn't only her going mad, but that her suspicions were completely justified. There had been some moments when she had wondered if she was suffering from a paranoiac insanity. But it was certain now that Vera Boldt had planned to spend the day at Ryme, rifling through her clothes and indulging her husband and playing the chatelaine. For reasons she didn't stop to think about, she minded more about the clothes and the house than she did about Julius. Endless women had temporarily occupied Julius from time to time; but, until Vera, none had ever pretended to be her friend while they did it.

She allowed Julius a minute to dial Vera's number, and then she swept down on him. As she threw open the door of his study, he threw the receiver down. He made silent goldfish movements with his mouth and, for a moment, she said nothing. Then, in a voice ringed with sarcasm, she asked him who he had been talking to on the telephone.

Rather than tell her to mind her own business, he chanced a lie and told her that he had called the Bennets to thank them for lunch the day before. She said nothing, but went to the telephone and dialled the Bennet's number. Ned answered.

'Hello, Ned,' she said in an utterly normal voice, 'How are you? Yes, I'm fine. I'm in such a muddle today. Has Julius telephoned you yet to thank you? He hasn't? He is dreadful, he promised he would. Well, thank you. It was delicious. I don't know what it is some people have against couscous. You will give Hilda my love, won't you. There goes my last ten pence. Well, goodbye, darling, we'll see you on Sunday. 'Bye.'

Evelyn kept the receiver in her hand and redialled, her eyes fixed on Julius, who sat in his chair in a withered heap. She had never been in the possession of such a controlling anger. Her face was set hard, and a lemon-yellow tint of evil had come to her eyes. When she spoke again, her voice was hard and commanding. Julius watched the sequence of numbers that she dialled, helpless and desperate. Vera answered with her crooning come-hither voice and her affected girlish laugh, thinking it was Julius calling her back. Evelyn remained silent until Vera had condemned herself, and then she said a terrible thing. Something that was so unlike my beloved Evelyn that I can hardly bear to repeat it. But the circumstances were, to some extent, a justification. She said, 'This is Evelyn, actually. I suppose you were expecting Julius.'

'Oh, Evelyn. Oh, my God. Oh, hi. Darling – how are you?'

'Don't you darling me, darling. I just wanted to let you know that although you may be accustomed to flashing your cunt around the rest of Somerset, you won't be doing it in my house.'

Vera began, in a patronising croon, to say to her, 'My God, Evelyn, I know how you must be feeling. Can't we talk?' Vera was an old hand at these situations. In a way, she enjoyed them almost as much as the actual affair. But halfway through her gambit, Evelyn told her to go and fuck herself and put the phone down.

Julius was immobile no longer. The fairest flower of his heart had been affronted. No one should be allowed to speak to Vera in that way. He leapt to his feet, shouting, 'How dare you!'

Evelyn answered by clenching her right fist and swinging it in the general direction of his face. She broke: his glasses; his nose; her little finger. He howled. She marched out of the room.

It was from then on that hell broke loose, mainly at night. Neither of them slept for the week that followed. The shouting and weeping was intermingled with the smashing of china. Evelyn, who had acquired a little pragmatism in her years with Julius, always made sure that the breakable object was either something that she didn't like or something that belonged to his family, before she threw it. And she collected the pieces afterwards to crock her geraniums. For the first time in their marriage, the struggle between them was approaching equality.

Evelyn and Julius were not the same couple that we saw in the Bennet's sitting-room four years ago. In the time from that moment when Evelyn first stopped believing every word that came from Julius, she had become a stronger, a more independent woman. She had detached herself from Julius. She no longer needed his good opinion, his approbation for everything that she did; and because she no longer needed it, he could no longer have power over her by withholding it. Since they had moved to Ryme, she had had the thinking time, in all those thousands of hours of gardening, to review her state, to conduct a mental analysis of Julius. She had decided that, although she probably could not do without it, it was possible that she could manipulate him to the same extent that he had always manipulated her.

It may in fact have been this palpable coldness towards him that had driven Julius into the arms of Vera Boldt. At the very least it had given Vera Boldt her opening. Julius was at that time ripe for adventure.

Neither was Julius the man we have seen at the hub of the cultural universe. He was beyond his depth, in a place where his character was impracticable, and so he had changed, and withdrawn before his circumstances.

The wistful, romantic side of Julius, which had been dormant for most of his life, had been called upon to assume the major role in his personality. He had been confident that this disinterested free-spirit was his true self. It was the self that was revealed to him under the influence of hallucinogenic substances in California. He was always convinced that, given the right circumstances, a literary guru would emerge. These delusions had carried him through and helped the success of his early life.

Perhaps he was right. Perhaps he had simply judged the circumstances wrongly. He had thought that Evelyn, once in the country and without her career, would revert to the biddable disciple he seemed to remember she had been before her fame and fortune. He was wrong. He found that, once her wings had been clipped, he lost her completely. She no longer made any attempt at communication. In that vast house, rather than be a comfort to him, she left him in complete isolation.

And the country. He thought that in the country one could do as one pleased. He had no idea that the occupation of a large house entailed duties and obligations. He was unaware of the expectations that the local people had of him, and so failed to play the part. Even if he had been aware of how he should have behaved, it is doubtful whether he would have been up to the similitude of it. So when it became plain to him, as it must have, that he was hated by the entire population of Ryme Episcopi, he was, if anything, surprised and hurt. He decided, like many a townsman before him, that country people were vicious and xenophobic. He couldn't see that Evelyn was well-liked in the village simply because she knew how to talk to people.

And Ryme, his castle in fairyland, shrank at his touch. Nothing that he planted would grow, and anything that he chopped down would spring again from the ground. It had become Evelyn's house. In a way that he could sense, it excluded him. He felt as though he was only a tentatively accepted visitor in his own fantasy.

HUGH LONGFORD, FROM his rooftop, knowing nothing of their history, observed them in this state: a miserable misfit of a man fading to silliness, and a self-possessed woman on the threshold of the best part of her life. Because they fought by night and rested by day, and because the South Cottage was out of shouting distance, he was unaware of the current violence, and so it was in all innocence that, about a week after hell broke loose, he asked Evelyn if she and Julius would like to come to supper.

The invitation was sociably meant and sociably accepted. Hugh went into Bruton and bought a brace of pheasants and plenty of wine and potatoes. He spent the afternoon making a chocolate roulade, amused at the ease with which bourgeois values could overcome him. Less cosy scenes were unfolding elsewhere.

Vera Boldt chose to confess her affection for Julius to Paul that afternoon. I can't say why. Perhaps she was bored. In any case, her confession misfired slightly. Usually, she could manage to twist it around so that it was Paul who felt guilty for driving her into a state of mind where she needed to have (what she termed) friendships with other men in order to preserve her sanity. She had long convinced Paul of his emotional inadequacy, and established her right to have recourse to (what she termed) counselling from other sources. This time, it wouldn't wear. He had had enough. He beat her up, not terribly seriously considering his strength, and threw her out of the house. He then felt better about Vera than he had done since before they were married. In his simple way, he decided that he had found happiness.

Vera, in defeat, made straight for the Bennet's kitchen table, where shelter and sympathy awaited her. Ned Bennet was a great listener. It is the only thing to be if you want to know everything. Vera sobbed uncontrollably for half an hour and then, lifting her eyes in watery innocence to Ned, and commanding all of her capacity for tender selflessness, she said, 'Oh, what if he tries to kill poor Julius?'

The dramatic possibilities of this were too much for Ned Bennet.

'We must save him!' he cried, as he rushed to the telephone.

'Oh Ned, you're such a true friend,' she crooned, before subsiding back into her grief.

'Julius?' said Ned.

'No,' said Evelyn, 'it's Evelyn.'

'Evelyn. Look. There's no time to explain. Paul Boldt is coming round there any minute and he says that he is going to kill Julius. He's gone completely mad. He's practically put Vera in the hospital. Warn Julius quickly. Have you got a gun in the house?'

'No,' said Evelyn.

'Perhaps it's better you haven't. In that case, just tell Julius to get away as quickly as possible.'

'I'll tell him,' said Evelyn.

'Poor you,' said Ned. 'Still, it can't be unexpected. It's just like the plot of one of your novels. Perhaps you could use it in the next one.'

'It would be a shame to let it go to waste,' said Evelyn.

She put the phone down and went to tell Julius. 'Ned Bennet just phoned to say that Paul Boldt is coming here to kill you.' Her voice was flat as she said it. She felt as though this development had nothing to do with her. It was Julius's problem.

She never thought, in all her time as a writer and commentator, that words simply spoken could have such an electrifying effect on someone. She knew that Julius was the greatest of cowards; Paul Boldt was a massively built man of a primitive disposition; there was some reason for enmity between them, but it seemed to her that there could never be reason for taking a statement of Ned Bennet's as seriously as this.

Julius went into a screaming panic. He flew about the house, locking doors and barring shutters and bolting windows. Ryme was the sort of house that was too big and old ever to be locked effectively, but in the space of nine minutes that evening, Julius made a fair job of it.

He told her to collect enough things for the night and put on her coat and get in the car.

'Where are we going?' she asked.

'To your brother's. He will never think of looking for us there.'

'What about Hugh?' she asked.

'Hugh?'

'Hugh the thatcher. We were going to have supper with him.'

'Oh God!' he said. 'I must warn him. You get in the car while I'm gone.'

She obeyed. She was bemused by him. Swept up in his panic. Without thinking, she put her tooth and hair brush together and went to get into the car.

Hugh was standing in the kitchen of the South Cottage with his hand up a pheasant's backside, when there was an anxious tapping on the glass pane of the door. Beyond it, the terrorised face of Julius could be made out, mouthing and signalling in the night. Then the door opened, and the face appeared in the room, white as a stage ghost. Julius said, in a horror-laden squeak, 'I'm afraid we can't come to supper tonight.'

Hugh said, 'Hello.'

'I am, awfully sorry,' Julius said, and he made to go away again. He was plainly in a hurry. But then he stopped and blurted, 'There is a very angry man coming here. When he comes, you mustn't let him in. I have locked the big house up and, if I were you, I'd lock the cottage and pretend you are not here. Better still, go out.'

'Who is he?' said Hugh. He gesticulated, with the bird still on his hand like a baseball mitt.

'If you see him you will know him,' called Julius as he began to trot away from the door. '*He is very angry*!' He screamed this last sentence as he dashed away into the darkness, like the victim of a Hammer film.

In the vacuum of puzzlement left to him, Hugh put all the food away and stood about uncertainly, battered by curiosity, peering from one window to the other, like Jack waiting for a tremble in the beanstalk. He decided that the South Cottage was too far away from where the main action might be, and so he decided to go and see what was happening in the darkness beyond the cottage. His blood was up, and he left the place at an excited sprint, with visions of coming across the strangled body of Julius in the shrubbery, or the towering angry man wreaking his havoc. He wondered if Julius had been killed (it had been plain that Julius was in fear of his life) and, if so, whether Evelyn would want to go on with the thatching of the Long Barn.

Evelyn, at that moment, was braced into the passenger seat of Julius's car as he hurtled down the drive of Ryme at sixty-three miles an hour. The violence of his driving dispelled her complacent bemusement. When he changed gear without braking, to take the turn at the gates, she suddenly screamed at him to stop, which he did with such force that she almost broke through the seat belt.

'This is the most completely stupid position I have ever been in,' she hissed at him, trying at the same time to catch her breath. 'I want to get out.'

Without saying a word, he leaned across her and opened her door and then, with both hands, he pushed her out of the car and on to the road with more force than she had realised was in him. At the same moment he accelerated so that the car was already taking off up the hill before she was even out of it.

Evelyn gathered herself up for a minute or two. Her anger and the sudden sharpness of the air prevented her from bursting into tears. The strap of her bra had snapped as she was hurled from the car; her knees were grazed through the stockings, and her ribs ached where she had hit the seat belt. She clasped her coat around her as though it wasn't just against the cold but in case someone might see her lopsidedness out here in the dark. She stood for minutes and minutes, thinking that to go back to the house alone would be the end of her; would begin something inevitable which she had been dreading. She couldn't bear the thought of an evening of tears. She thought of walking to the pub in Ryme Episcopi, but felt too vulnerable to go there alone. Like a Victorian heroine, she felt at that moment that her composure came first. Her composure, not as a first line of defence but as the only thing left to her. Drawing her head back and stiffening herself, as though she was surrounded by a watching crowd, she allowed an automaton to take her over and, while this *doppelgänger* was in

93

control, she remembered Hugh Longford and his supper invitation.

Hugh had gone out, leaving his door wide open so as not to make the man even angrier than he was by obstructing him. It was a clear, dry and cold night. Starry and sharp. It snapped the breath as it came out of his mouth and, before he had exhaled three times, he was taken over by the air and the night. He almost forgot Julius and the angry man, and left them behind on the threshold of the cottage. He walked off among the trees, deafened with the noise his boots made on the breaking grass, and if he stopped, the air was spiked with silence. He crossed through the wood and the garden in his own time, dispersing the rabbits as he came upon them. The terms and the boundary were before him, and beyond was the hill paddock full of the sound of the horses breathing and the crackling of their frosted rugs as they walked about. Hugh wandered up the field like a dazed man, stumbling over tussocks because of looking at the stars.

As he reached the hedge by the road, it occurred to him to climb through it and make his way back by a circular route. He climbed to the bank and began to weave his way through the bullfinch.

While he was caught in the branches, a roar of car engine came up to him from the direction of the drive, and headlights streaked through the dark below. The car skidded to a stop in the gateway and screeched off again almost at once.

He waited, suspended in the hedge like a fly in a web, for the car to pass him. It climbed the hill at a reckless speed. Up the hill from Hugh, a hare in the road froze in its headlights. Within the car, Julius's manic face was picked out in the lights of the dash, blind to the hare and senseless to the hare's death scream.

The hare was run over and the car sped away, the unshut passenger door flapping at the bends. Hugh disentangled himself out of the hedge and went over to where the corpse lay. He poked his foot at it and wondered what to do with it, as though it was his responsibility or as though it had some significance.

He thought that he should bring it back, without knowing why: he might be able to eat it himself or he might feed it to Evelyn's cats.

Carrying the hare by the ears he went back the way he came rather than by the road, as though there was a reason to be back as quickly as he could. Once he was in the field, he began to run, beginning to think again about the angry man, and whether he had been and gone and whether he had missed him. He ran in leaps down the hill, each drop-stride sending a bolt through his body, and the heat of running building up inside of him, and the hare dancing maniacally in his hand. In his speed, he took off ten feet from the bottom and sailed over the boundary, changing legs on top like a horse.

Once he was back within the cottage and the light, he viewed the sweat and mud and the blood of the animal that spattered him and, leaving the hare to drip in the sink, he went to the shower to wash himself.

He was back in the kitchen, drying himself down with a towel before the electric heater, when a knock came to the door and another face peered at him through the glass.

Without giving him time to wonder if it was the angry man and so defend himself, and barely giving him the time to pull the towel about his middle, Evelyn pushed the door open and, seeming to be unconscious of his state, strode into the room as though she had a pack of elkhounds at her heels. The collar of her winter coat stood up about her ears, and her face was cross and overbearing. She cast a shrivelling look down her nose at him, and pulled the coat tighter about her as though the room was infected.

Hugh Longford knotted his small towel as casually as he could manage and tightened his stomach a little.

'Is your invitation to supper still open?' she asked him in a provokingly superior voice. He could feel his back stiffening and an arrogance equal to hers taking him over, in place of the dignity he had lost.

'Of course,' he said. 'I have just been running, but I will put it in the oven as soon as I am dressed.'

She looked mildly shocked, as though he shouldn't have drawn attention to his nakedness. She had left the door open behind her; the cottage was below freezing and his flesh was beginning to resemble the surface of a golfball, and he hoped that she would go before his knees started to knock. For where would his dignity be then?

She said, 'It is terribly cold in here. I think we should eat at the big house. Don't you?' Her question had more of the tone of a command than a request to it.

He went on trying to behave like a man at a cocktail party, and said to her in a conversational tone, 'It can be quite warm in here, when the door is shut.' He needn't have spoken. She brushed him aside in the middle of his sentence, and announced that she would go and lay the table at the big house.

'And,' she added, meaning to have a parting shot, 'as you are so good at running, perhaps you could just run to the pub and get a bottle of wine.'

She made a sweeping turn to leave the room, thinking that her performance was over. That her dignity was intact: she had overcome her fall and her broken strap and the ridiculousness of the position into which she had been put.

But it was only now that the ridiculousness of it struck Hugh. As she turned her back, he called after her in his normal voice, in the voice of their friendship, 'There's no need for that.' She stopped and turned to him again. Her mask and the collar of her coat had fallen. He continued, 'I have plenty of wine already. I'll just bring some from here.'

She said in her soft old voice, 'I'll pay you for it. I'll pay you back later.'

'Don't be silly,' he said, 'wait a second.' He dashed upstairs, and she stood, nervously, as he clumped about over her head. He reappeared in a minute or two, decently, warmly clad. 'Tell me,' he said, 'you don't have to if you don't want to. It may seem like none of my business, but if I'm to be murdered in my bed by him, I'd feel happier to know who this angry man is.'

'Oh that,' she said, throwing it away from her as if it were a small irritation. 'He isn't going to bother you. It's only a neighbour whose wife Julius has been having an affair with.'

She said it as if she had no reason to mind it. As if it was a thing which Julius did regularly with her full acquiescence. Something which became a bore when the cuckolded husband took umbrage. She spoke as if there was nothing to be gained by anyone referring to it again.

'Oh I see,' said Hugh, 'if that's all it is.'

She said she would see him later, and went away into the dark towards the big house with her coat collar limp over her shoulders.

In Hugh's mind, the angry man had declined into a dim and boring prospect. His knowledge of the English as a race was limited, but he knew from their newspapers that adultery was as common amongst them as hot dinners, and that there was nothing strange or exiting about an open marriage, such as Julius and Evelyn seemed to have. He wondered, in the wake of Evelyn's leaving, whether it was her intention to seduce him that night, and he wondered if he would be tempted to accommodate her. He had not had his bed to himself for long enough yet to be mourning the gap between him and the wall. For the last two months he had been celebrating his independence and glorying in his isolation each morning as he woke. There had been pangs of loneliness from time to time, but these were nothing compared with the luxury of having no one to satisfy but himself.

A year ago, it would not have been a question of temptation. Nothing would have prevented him from leaping straight into such an interesting and complicated situation as the Ryme marriage. But, since then, he had acquired new values, and the charms of a life without sex and skulduggery had yet to pall.

And, behind all this, was his premonition that Evelyn was something more to him than an acquaintance. He had an instinct about her that held him back for the moment; that placed her in the role of an inviolable friend, for the time being.

He dressed properly, and walked through the wood to the big house, thinking that he was ready for anything. He brought his pheasants and his potatoes and her wine, looking forward to an evening with Evelyn and without Julius being awkward all over the place.

Of course, Paul Boldt never did make an appearance. His primitive mind was still concerned solely with Vera. He had loved her and trusted her and seen her as perfect for half of his life. It was the greatest of blows to him to have to countenance the possibility that she might be flawed.

By the time that Hugh had found his way into the kitchen of the big house, Evelyn had lost all trace of arrogance and competence, and she was sitting at her kitchen table, utterly normal. He opened the wine for her and he cooked for them, and she apologised to him, saying that she was sorry they had put his evening out.

He, only out of honesty, said no, it was better this way and, indeed, her kitchen was so much warmer than the South Cottage could ever hope to be.

He did most of the talking and ate all of the food. She listened, eating nothing, but drank a lot, without effect. She asked the odd leading question, out of politeness, and by the time they had finished, he had told her just about everything that he was prepared to let anyone know. He hadn't spoken at length to anyone for a long time, and what he said came out with that compressed force and honesty that is built up in silence.

He realised, not long after he had sat down at that table, that there was no question of anyone seducing anyone that evening. It was two in the morning before he had finished, and he was in his bed and she was in hers. In the dark, and the quiet vacuum left by the sound of his own voice, he thought about Julius and Evelyn, and nothing would fall into place.

She, who seemed warm and vulnerable, seemed out of place in that cold modern marriage. She, whose books were full of women destroyed by their husbands' callousness, seemed an unlikely candidate to be flourishing in this hard atmosphere. And if it was an open marriage, what, then, sustained it? There was no empathy apparent between the protagonists. They seemed to have nothing in common that he could see. For hours he lay awake, trying to puzzle out the convenience that bound them together.

THE WINTER PROGRESSED, grew colder and darker, became, inevitably, more like Christmas. Nothing was resolved at the big house. Julius was still in love and trying to get Evelyn to see it his way, and Evelyn was still fighting for her own survival. She had begun, in a small way, to talk to Hugh. She brought coffee to him in the middle of the morning, and he would come down from his roof and wrap his magenta hands about the mug and they would sit on the mounting block and gossip. She began to value the calmness and normality of their friendship, as a foil to the high drama of the rest of their life.

On some afternoons, while he was still working, she would go and tidy the South Cottage for him; heaping his batchelorhood into tidier piles and leaving pots of marmalade in his cupboard. At other times she was supposed to be editing the anthology of women's prose but, when she attempted it, she found herself staring blankly at a sheet of paper, feeling the cracks in her life become larger and more intricate.

Once, Julius found her coming out of the South Cottage. He asked her, in a furious voice, what she had been doing. She couldn't be bothered to answer him, and left him furious among the trees. She knew that, no matter how it all turned out, she had grown on from Julius. She had no concept of how her life could be without him, the habit of living with him was so deep, but a life with him was beginning to seem a hollow exercise. Her reasons for doing anything at all were growing thinner. She could only follow her instincts and salvage her self-possession where she could lay hold of it.

The approach of Christmas brought the children down. Evelyn still referred to them as the children, although they were approaching their mid-twenties by now. Evelyn told Hugh that it would be nice for him to have people his own age to talk to for a change. Once the children came down, she retreated from his company, feeling sure that he only spoke to her for want of a more suitable companion.

Hugh met the children in the pub at Ryme Episcopi. There was Benedict, whom he could meet as an old friend, and Hannah, whom he hadn't met, and her boyfriend. Although he knew Benedict quite well, he realised that, as a group, the children were foreign to him. He had seen their like at railway stations in Italy and in Hampstead cafés. They were the children of progressive education. Confident in their politics, which were broadly left wing, and sure in their opinions of art and literature, and careless of the chic they took for granted. Hugh watched them as a spectacle, and listened to their heated discussions of even who should play against whom at snooker.

He felt for the moment that he could have nothing to say to them. He knew they would disapprove of hunting and be ignorant of the countryside, and that their knowledge of books and music would be so broad as to exclude him. He could see that they were all on a stage because the pub was a foreign atmosphere to them. They spoke too loudly, and in voices that, in Benedict's case at least, he knew were not their own.

Their argument over the playing of snooker entranced him. It gave the pub the feel of a socialist committee room. Their cases were eloquently and passionately put, but without any animosity or sundering of their unity as outsiders in a foreign medium.

The children went home from the pub first, leaving him on his own and without any inclination to indulge the landlord by relieving the boredom of his vigil. He followed them within minutes.

The night was sharp. It was the first really cold night of the winter, the first intimation of weeks of arctic weather. There was a dangerous edge to the air; a hardness that scraped on your skin. It would be too cold for thatching, and possibly there would be snow as well. Hugh walked home, knowing he was about to be on holiday, wondering whether to stay at Ryme or to risk going home, and being trapped there for the whole of Christmas.

As he passed the barn on his way to the cottage, he could make out the figure of Benedict Cotton standing restlessly beneath the untrimmed eaves without a coat on him. He didn't seem to notice the cold, but had an air of tragedy to his attitude. As Hugh approached, he stepped forward.

'Are you all right?' Hugh asked, almost involuntarily.

'I'm a bit troubled, actually,' he replied, in an unexpectedly vulnerable tone of voice. Hugh offered him coffee, and they walked in silence together to the South Cottage. They sat in the kitchen, drinking tea, in fact, and talked over Benedict's troubles which centred around his girlfriend who was dying of cancer. Could die any moment.

Hugh could think of nothing to say, but it was plain by his expression that he was someone who might sympathise, and they were both still young enough to allow talk to be unselfconscious. Hugh thought for a moment that this was his role, to be analyst of the Cotton family.

Hugh Longford, who in his previous life had always been a man to go drinking with, and a man to be relied upon to electrify the people around him with his wildness and his charm, was never the sort of man you would go to if you needed to pour your soul out over tea. Standing back from himself that night while Benedict was talking, he was surprised and amused by this new use which people seemed to be making of him. And, at the same time that he was concerned about and pained for Benedict, he was elated by the intimacy and the power of emotion and by his own power in being the man to help the troubles of another.

When Benedict left to go to his bed in the big house, he left Hugh Longford drained and dry, aching from the flexion of a previously unused muscle. And, when it was dark, and Hugh Longford was still and sleepless in his bed, tears began to course from his eyes, running through the channels of his ears, and all for no reason that he could think of. He could never remember weeping before in all his life, and now it came to him for no reason, it seemed, at all.

He did go home for Christmas, and had the same dreadful

Christmas that he had always had, and it was hard to get away, because he could give no reason to anyone for wanting to get away, and so he stayed until nearly the New Year with no heart for staying, and everyone who flattered themselves they knew him shook their heads and said he was only a ghost of his former self. As for himself, he knew that it was his former self that haunted him.

Sick of being surrounded by people, he arrived back in Ryme on the afternoon of New Year's Eve. He saw Benedict in the distance, but only waved to him. Exhausted by home, he went to bed early, without waiting for twelve or thinking of it. He no longer amazed himself by doing these things.

At the big house, the crescendo was reaching its climax. Julius had been wanting to move Vera in, but Evelyn refused to move out; refused to accommodate them in any way, saying that Julius would only get her out by selling the house. That that scheming cow was only interested in the house, in any case. See if she still loves you when you are living in a cottage.

Julius offered her one of the cottages rent-free for life; he said that the house was so enormous, couldn't she live in one end while he and Vera occupied the other; live like civilised people should. How could she be so selfish as to pervert the course of true love.

It was the course of true love now. At first it had been, 'I need her as a friend. I have problems and she seems to be the only one who can understand them. You have never given me my due. You have never given me credit for any sensitivity. Never seen that I could be an artist. You have no understanding of art; of the artist in me. I need the help she can give me, and then our marriage will be better, if only you allow us the space until I am sorted out.'

His admitting of anything had progressed from that, in stages through, 'I have never been truly in love before,' and on to the current climate of free-for-all ultimatums.

By New Year's Eve, when Hannah and her boyfriend had gone back to London, and there was only Benedict away in the other end of the house, wrapped up in his own concerns, there was nothing that could be said that hadn't been, hadn't been screamed and hissed and conveyed at every tone between.

When the pealing of churchbells from Ryme Episcopi came round the hills to Ryme, they found Evelyn sitting at the foot of a term beneath the ilex in the woods, numb to the cold with her grief and in a corridor of her own sorrow. Her head rested against the tree, and she was watching the term smiling in the moonlight and the frost glittering on her bulging sandstone cheek. All the time she was weeping. But that was something she hardly noticed now. Weeping seemed a normal state, preferable to hysterics.

The bells from Ryme Episcopi woke Hugh in his bed, and the moment he woke he was miserable. He then understood that you don't gather to celebrate the New Year. That it is only to forget, to ignore what a desolate occasion the New Year is.

Afterwards, when they were together and they talked about that evening, it seemed like stupidity to them that at midnight they had been no more than thirty yards apart and each unaware of the other's desolation.

Julius left her on New Year's Day. He went without warning and said that he didn't know where he would be, perhaps the south of France, he needed to think. And so he just vanished, went off to decide whether he was more in love with Vera or with his circumstances at Ryme.

Hugh spent the day at Lyme Regis. He went to see the place where Louisa Musgrove had fallen from the Cobb. He could think of no better reason for going anywhere else on a day as empty as that one.

When he came back in the afternoon, his mind cleared and sorted, he found a note addressed to him on his kitchen table.

It read, 'Julius has left my mum, and she is in a pretty bad way and I wonder if you could just see she is all right. I have to go to London. Angela is dead. Sorry to load all this on to you, Ben.'

Hugh panicked and ran to the big house with visions of empty Mogadon bottles and locked bathroom doors. He didn't bother to knock, only went straight to the main hall before he came to a stop, and began to wonder what next.

He went back to the door and put his finger to the bell. Outside, it was still afternoon, but in the hall the dusk was gathering. He heard the noise of a door closing from somewhere up in the house, and so he went back to the bottom of the staircase and called her name. Each time he called, his voice caught slightly in the back of his throat. He called twice and, by the second time, she had appeared in the gloom at the top of the stairs, like Lucia de Lammermoor, all hair and nightclothes, clutching the rail, not so much that she might fall down the stairs, but that she might float away from them.

'Are you all right?' he asked, almost involuntarily.

'Julius has gone,' she said. Her voice implied that she wasn't. He asked her again if she was all right, and she said yes. Yes – she apologised and said she had taken a sleeping tablet. He asked her if she was going to be all right. She said yes.

'I am sorry,' she said, 'I will just go back to bed now.'

Hugh agreed, all reluctance. The light was dimming moment by moment, and what he could see of her was fading in it. It strained his eyes to maintain the picture he had of her, reduced to her essence by grief. In the long interval since he had last seen her, all her fat and all her pretence and all her comfort had fallen away. Hugh looked at her and saw a creature as dispossessed of her past as himself, saw someone not unlike himself.

The snow had started up when he went back outside, flinging itself around in fat, cold circles. He hardly noticed. He was thinking about Evelyn and nothing else.

Morning and night he ministered to her. He went to the pub for her and brought her gin and wine and drank it with her. Because she refused to eat anything at all, he watched her grow alarmingly thin. While they talked and drank, she would cook him fishcakes on the Aga and watch him eat them. Several times she said she was grateful to him for putting up with her, and he said that he didn't know what she was talking about.

There was a day when he came in to take his place among the cats on the kitchen table, and he was stopped in his tracks by a diminutive woman who stood before the Aga with her arms stretched along the rail of it and her head cocked on one side with an expression of the deepest concern on her face. Her square-cut jet hair hung out across her face and the cold weather had brought her out in clothes from the early Seventies and a large Peruvian poncho that most people would have been grateful to have lost. She was in the process of trying to overpower Evelyn's tragedy with what she chose to consider her own level-headedness.

'But darling,' she was saying, 'won't you just talk to Vera. Vera will talk to you. She really still wants to be your friend.'

Evelyn was sitting at the table, behind a circlet of her cats, beating mayonnaise for the sake of her composure.

'I'll bet she does,' she said.

Hilda Bennet leaned further forward from the Aga, in an attitude that might have been charming in a schoolgirl and, summoning all the compassion and understanding that her manner could muster, said indulgently to Evelyn, 'But darling what *do* you want to do?'

Evelyn stopped her beating for a moment of reflection, and then continued without saying a word.

Hilda Bennet persisted. 'How do you feel about Vera? I could go now and bring her here. What would you do if she were here? Would you talk to her?'

'No,' said Evelyn. 'If she came anywhere near me I would probably hit her. As hard as I could.'

Hugh Longford felt that he had stood in the door long enough and it was time they were aware of his presence. He sniffed aloud and walked further into the room. Hilda, on noticing him, gave him a look that was fleetingly malevolent. She resented his interruption. Just as she thought she was about to raise Evelyn's consciousness.

Evelyn, once she had smiled her greeting at him, seemed to be unaffected by his presence. He suspected that she had taken a Valium.

'Oh Hugh,' she said, 'this is Hilda Bennet. Have you met? Hilda kindly came to see if I was all right.'

'It's the least I can do, darling. No, I don't think we have met.'

'Yes, we have,' said Hugh. 'We met at the Kopses in Ryme Epsicopi. In October.'

Hilda looked at him closely, before admitting to the possibility that she might have met him at the Kopses. She met so many young men at the Kopses these days. She supposed it was all those daughters they had.

'Probably,' said Hugh.

Hilda turned from him, and resumed her chief business.

'Darling, we can't just leave it like this. You could all meet at my house. You and Julius and Vera. You could all have a lovely supper and sort this out. How do you feel about that?'

She was leaning so far forward from the Aga rail, in her

earnestness, that Evelyn felt compelled to answer her, if only to prevent her from falling.

'I am sure you are being kind. I know you are doing what you think is best. But, if I see Vera, I will kill her.'

'Poor darling,' said Hilda.

Evelyn got up from the table and went into the pantry where she began to rummage around in the freezer. Hilda watched after her for a moment and then, bestowing a look of complete familiarity and confidence on Hugh, as if they were old friends and she expected him to sympathise with her cause, said, 'What do *you* think? The poor thing is so upset that she hardly knows what she is saying. But all of them really must talk it out, you know. I've done my best. Do you know Vera?'

'Only by reputation,' said Hugh.

'She is terribly nice, you know. She and Evelyn were the greatest of friends. It's so sad that all of this had to happen.' She spoke in her normal voice, as though Evelyn wasn't only in the next room and couldn't hear every word. She spoke as though the whole incident had been as inevitable as the weather and had been nobody's fault. She couldn't help adding, in a cheerful voice, 'But I expect it will be all for the best, once we sort it out and Evelyn and Vera are friends again.'

'There aren't many people I would go to prison for killing,' Evelyn interjected from the freezer, 'and Vera is one of them.'

'The poor thing,' Hilda said to Hugh, wrinkling her nose at him as though one of them was a child. 'Darling,' she called, swooping into her hanging position, 'I have to go in a minute. Is there nothing I can do for you? I could have Vera here in a moment. She really does want to make up with you.'

Evelyn reappeared. 'Gloat over her conquest do you mean? Perhaps she is coming to make an inventory of the fittings. Or to steal some more of my clothes.'

'Oh, darling,' said Hilda. 'I do wish I could help you more. Do you want anything from Bruton? I could easily drop it in on my way back.'

Evelyn said how kind it was, but no, there was nothing she could think of. Hilda began to take her leave, embracing Evelyn warmly, so that Evelyn began to cry. For a moment, an expression of compassion crossed Hilda's face that seemed to be genuine. She left Evelyn in a heap and Hugh saw her to her car.

'You will see that she is all right, won't you?' she said to Hugh.

'I don't have anything else to do,' he said.

He returned to Evelyn and found her separating fishcakes that had been frozen together, using a sharp knife. She couldn't see properly with her watery eyes, and so he took the knife from her before she hurt herself.

'I'm sorry,' she said. 'She was pretending to be my friend. That was the worst, in a way.'

'Hilda?' he said, puzzled.

'Hilda? No, Not Hilda. Hardly her. Hilda is terribly sweet, but I don't think she has the intelligence to betray someone. No, I mean Vera. She spent most of the summer in this house. She convinced me that she was my best friend. All the time she was plotting to steal everything I have. If it was only Julius. That would be fine. As far as I am concerned now, anyone is welcome to Julius. But she is trying to steal my whole life. She wants this house. She wants my friends. She has even been stealing my clothes. Did I tell you that? There was a dress, not a wonderful dress, but a dress she had always admired. I couldn't find it. I said to Julius that bitch has been stealing my clothes. He denied it, but today I saw that the dress was back in my wardrobe. With a cleaning ticket pinned to it. I've never had it dry-cleaned. The bitch. She wants everything.'

'Did you like her? said Hugh.

She looked at him as though she had no understanding of what the words meant. He could see, by watching her eyes, the phases of mind she was passing through before she was ready with her answer.

'Did you like her?' he persisted.

'She was always trying to be my friend,' said Evelyn. 'I don't know what you would think of her if you met her. Perhaps you would think she was wonderful. Everyone else seems to. She can be very charming.'

Hugh remembered the time when he had seen Julius and what must have been Vera Boldt from the roof of the Long Barn. He was about to tell Evelyn, but he thought the better of it. In her current state of mind he didn't want to be accused of membership of a conspiracy of silence against her. At present she needed

107

someone who was completely on her side. Someone from the outside who would know nothing except what she might choose to say.

'No,' he said. 'I don't think so. She doesn't sound like someone I would like at all.'

'How would you know?' she said, but she was pleased with what he had said. More cheerful for his loyalty.

'I am brilliant at judging characters,' he said.

'Even the ones you have never met,' she said.

'It is an instinct,' he said.

She smiled at him. That subject was finished for the moment. They stayed in silence for a while. For such a long while that he began to feel awkward. She heaved the frying pan on to the Aga for his fishcakes.

'Are you fond of Hilda Bennet?' he asked her, if only to break the silence.

'Hilda,' she said. 'Hilda is very kind. I've known her for a long time. Since the early Sixties.'

'Are you fond of her?' he said.

'She isn't a best friend. No. Hilda is the sort of woman who would drive you to John o' Groat's to see your sick mother, and as soon as you arrived she would go back to Land's End to collect your children for you, and then come back to John o' Groat's to bring you home for tea.'

'I'd rather take the train,' said Hugh.

'You don't like her?'

'It's an instinct,' he said.

'Poor Hilda,' said Evelyn.

'The Kopses can't stand her. Susan Kopse says that she is inclined to barge in. A bit of a meddler.'

'If you think Hilda is a meddler then you haven't met her husband,' said Evelyn.

'I have,' he said.

'Then you should have more sympathy for her.' Evelyn spoke as if she was correcting him. As if he had threatened to come beyond a line that was still drawn in her mind.

He was embarrassed by this ticking-off. He concentrated hard on picking his fingernails for a few moments, until his embarrassment turned to slight crossness. What should stop him expressing an opinion?

'All I meant,' he said, 'was that I have met more sensitive women in my time. And, after all, she seems to be more Vera's friend than yours.'

It was only when he had said this that he could see what was happening. That there was a battle for friendships going on between Evelyn and Vera, that friends, like everything else in the divorce, would have to be divided. That Evelyn was hanging on to as many of them as she possibly could, if for no other reason than denying them to Vera.

'I'm sorry,' he said.

'No,' she said. 'You were right. But it isn't Hilda's fault. None of this can be very easy for anyone. It must be so boring for anyone else. In a way, it is nice to have people like Hilda Bennet who are plainly so thrilled by the whole thing. It makes me less guilty about talking to them for hours.' She went on poking the fishcakes with her back to him. Then she looked at him with all the misery gone from her face, replaced by a look of malicious amusement, and she said, 'The other thing is, I suppose, that I can be sure of anything I say to Hilda going straight back to Vera Boldt. It's a direct line to the enemy camp.'

In the days that followed, her independence of mind gradually increased. For every three steps forward there would be two back. On some days he would come in to find her fallen apart, wailing that she had never been on her own before. That she had always been supported by someone.

'I'm sure someone will want you,' he would tell her gruffly.

'I am too old,' she would wail.

'Then you will have to pay someone.'

He thought it was best to give no quarter to this self-pity. It usually worked. Usually he made her smile with his refusal to indulge her. Although once she said, 'With what? I have no money.'

'Well, make some. Write another book.'

'It isn't making it. It's managing it. Julius always managed the money. I am hopeless at that. I won't survive. I will be living on Victoria Station out of a carrier bag.'

'I bet it's a Harrods carrier bag,' he said.

'I am being serious,' she said.

'Physician, heal thyself,' he said.

'What do you mean?' she said.

'Oh, for God's sake,' he said. 'Every bookshop in this country and God knows where else is half-stuffed with books you have written exhorting female independence. All of your heroines managed it. Most of your readers have done it. Why can't you?'

She said nothing. She held her hair up to her face so that it covered the lower half like a veil. He thought he had pushed her too far.

'I'm sorry,' he said. And then, regretting this, he said, 'But I mean it.' He said it in a low voice, turning his head away from her at the same time.

'No,' she said. 'You are right. Of course you think that. Of course everyone does. People are surprised to know that there is a man in my life at all. I have no defence. Except how am I to know what it is to be a miserable housewife unless I am a miserable housewife?'

'You could use your imagination,' he said.

'I haven't got one,' she said.

'Bollux,' he said.

'Say that again,' she said.

'What?' he said.

'That word. I've never heard it said like that.'

'Don't patronise my accent,' he said.

'I'm not. I think it's very charming.'

'That's what I mean,' he said. 'You're avoiding the issue.'

'I don't know,' she said.

'Perhaps it is time you set about researching the second half of those books, the bit where the miserable housewife has her revenge and finds independence.'

'I don't know,' she said. 'That is the fantasy half. I don't actually believe all that. I only put it in to make everyone feel better at the end. I feel guilty in case anyone would commit suicide after reading it. I couldn't be responsible for anything but a happy ending.'

He looked at her and couldn't work out whether she was actually talking to him, or whether this was something she said to journalists. It was hard to see whether she meant it or not. He got up and said he had to go. 'I'll see you tomorrow,' he said.

She smiled and said it would be nice. He felt as though he was a stranger being dismissed from her presence.

110

THE NEXT DAY was bright and clear with strong sunshine and a false hint of spring in the wind. Hugh Longford woke late and exhausted, and lay for a while in his bed while the room was yellow with sunshine. He thought about Evelyn and found himself looking forward to seeing her. By the time he got up, he was in the grip of something close to elation. Whether it was the bright weather or the prospect of being with Evelyn he never stopped to think. Happiness is only likely to be analysed in sorrow.

When he washed himself he scrubbed himself. He shaved twice and brushed his teeth for double the time. He laughed at himself thinking that this was the difference between friendship and love. In love, people were supposed to accept him with an acrid smell and a three-day stubble because they loved him. He had no right to impose himself on a friend to that extent. He came out of the South Cottage feeling almost naked with cleanliness.

The door by which he usually entered the big house was locked. He was about to go and enter by another door, but instinct made him stay where he was and ring the bell. It was something of a shock to him when Julius answered.

'You're looking very smart,' said Julius. He was wreathed in smiles and indulgence. He was behaving as though he had never gone away, or as though it had only been a little holiday and that, now he was back, nothing had changed. Hugh was too shocked to say anything. Julius stepped outside the door as though they were going over to the barn to discuss it. He said, 'You haven't got very far in the last few weeks.'

'It hasn't really been the weather,' Hugh said. The last thing he wanted was to spend the rest of his morning talking about the barn roof with Julius. He realised, to his surprise, that he was irritated by Julius's return. He thought he should have been glad, for Evelyn's sake.

He told himself that it was for Evelyn's sake he wished Julius had stayed away, that Julius, in his opinion, was bad for Evelyn, that he had decided that the whole break-up was the best thing that could happen to her. But then he thought Who am I to decide all of this? What has it got to do with me? Why should I worry if he goes or stays? If he stays, I am more likely to get paid for the roof. These people, really, are nothing to me.

All of this had gone through his head in a second or two. It is amazing the speed at which a mind can work in a crisis. Julius had begun to walk towards the barn, expecting Hugh to follow. But instead he stood by the open door and said, 'Is Evelyn in?'

'Did you want to see her?' said Julius, rather sharply.

'I thought I would just say hello,' he said, as casually as he could manage.

'She is in her office,' said Julius. 'Do you know where that is?'

'I expect I will find it,' he said, and went into the house without waiting for directions.

He found Evelyn in her office. She and Hannah were crawling about the floor sorting sheaves of papers into bundles. The room was washed with the light of the day: pure and cold and cheerful and yellow. Evelyn wore a yellow woollen dress; a ribbed dress that stretched with her across the floor, showing every moment of her where it clung to her and fell away. By an illusion of the light, or a weakness of his mind, the light seemed to emanate from her and be passing through the windows to the outside, rather than the reverse. She was pleased to see him. She and Hannah both. Her eyes, when she looked at him in this light, were a shade of veined orange.

He sat in a chair among them as they bundled and rebundled the feminist anthology across the floor. He could see that nothing was actually being done, that work was being invented, perhaps to occupy Hannah and make her feel useful. Perhaps it was a flurry of industry to keep Julius at bay. It was even possible that they had no idea that they were not being deeply practical, and that they could see some progress in their shuffling. But, in any case, he allowed them to carry on because they were all talking as though they were three old friends, and because the morning seemed so pleasant and Julius could be forgotten while he was the other side of the door.

When lunchtime came he said that they should all go down to the pub in Ryme Priory. He meant the three of them. He had forgotten by now that Julius was back.

'You two go,' Evelyn said. 'I think Julius and I have to be in Bruton for lunch.'

She thought she was doing them a favour. She thought it was time that Hugh had someone his own age to talk to after weeks of listening to her moping and groaning. She thought that Hugh would be a distinct improvement on Hannah's previous boyfriend and she thought it would nice for Hannah if she lived in the country. By this stage, it had occurred to her once or twice to wish she had been at least fifteen years younger when she met him. That was as far as she had presumed to take her thoughts of him. Now, what had seemed fey to wish for herself seemed practical and kind to wish for Hannah. She packed them off to the pub, waving cheerily like Mrs Kirrin.

Julius asked Hannah if she would like to walk or be driven. She said she would walk, and they set out.

Once Hugh was out of Evelyn's presence, he became infected with the virus he had contracted while sitting near her. He became boyish and garrulous and physically explosive. He dashed about Hannah, unable to contain his over-excitement; not really knowing the reason for it, but thinking it might be the weather. He eventually settled to a pertinent tone of conversation, as though he knew her better than he did.

At first they talked of his work and of hers, and how awful it must be to have to live in London; and she said yes, how lovely it must be to live in the country.

Then, in the middle of it all, Hugh said that he was a bit surprised to see Julius back.

Hannah looked at him for a moment, trying to assess the depth of his involvement. Evelyn had said that the thatcher had been a help to her. He seemed to have become her friend. And the

113

directness of his question was irresistible. She decided that he was someone she could talk to.

She said, 'Yes, poor Evelyn.'

'Is he back for good, do you think?'

'I don't know,' she said. 'It isn't over. Last night was terrible. I couldn't get any sleep with all the screaming. It might have been better if I stayed in London.'

'Julius asked you to come down,' he said.

'Yes, he did. How did you know?'

'I am beginning to know Julius, and the way he operates.' He said this as they were going in through the door of the pub, and the transition from outdoors to in changed the conversation for a while. She had time to think about what he had said, but she could make no sense of it. All through the luncheon they talked of other things, until she began to feel that she knew him, or at least that she liked him, and that he had Evelyn's best interests at heart, and so she could trust him. By the time they stood up to walk home, with a fair quantity of warm alcohol running through them, she felt that she could talk to him. That she would have nothing to lose by honesty.

'What did you mean, about the way that Julius operates?' she asked him as they were passing again through the door where the conversation had been dropped.

Hugh tumbled to her innocence and he was irritated by it. She was playing Ann to her father's Uncle Quentin. She was taking her stepmother's lead in suppressing her intelligence with regard to Julius. Trying to keep the crossness out of his voice, Hugh said, 'I shouldn't have to explain that to you. He is your father. Surely you must have observed his character for yourself.' He looked at her, expecting her to release him from the obligation to go further. But she said nothing, and continued to regard him with the same degree of expectation, and so he continued, 'Julius is not the bravest man on this earth. He brought you down from London to shield himself from some of Evelyn's anger. You are here to act as a buffer.'

'I don't know if that is true,' she said.

He shrugged, and they continued walking. They were halfway from Ryme Priory to Ryme Episcopi, each waiting for a more benign subject to come and restore their conversation. But then the silence became awkward, and Hugh could see that there was nothing to be done but finish what was started.

'Do you like your father?' he asked her.

'What do you mean? Is it possible not to like your father?'

'I can't stand my father,' he said. 'That doesn't mean I don't love him. Loving him is a complication. But I don't have two words to say to him. If he wasn't related to me I don't see that I could have anything to do with him. I can't approve of him, nor does he look for my approval.' As he spoke he could feel himself running out of steam. He could feel that he and his father had no bearing on anything that was happening here. He heard his voice wind down and trail off in the last sentence. Hannah didn't even seem as though she was listening.

And then what she had been thinking of burst out of her, and she said to him, 'It is so irritating. How can Julius leave Evelyn for someone like Vera Boldt? How could he? Have you ever seen her? She is the opposite of everything that Evelyn is.'

'What is she like?' he said.

Hannah made an expression of disgust. She said, 'All my life I have tried to be like Evelyn. I always thought that Evelyn was perfect. And Vera is so scrawny and blonde and obvious. There is nothing soft about her. You know how voluptuous Evelyn is. There is all that generosity and softness. You know how soft her voice is. Sometimes, people can't tell us apart on the telephone. I feel that I am more like Evelyn than like my natural mother. How can Julius give her up for someone as angular and brash? How could he pretend for so long that he wanted someone like Evelyn, and then fall in love with someone like Vera?'

He thought about asking her if she felt that, in rejecting Evelyn, her father was also rejecting her, as someone who had modelled herself on Evelyn. But he decided that the question was too simplistic and Freudian and hurtful. So, instead, he said that he expected love was more complicated than that.

'And so, you are an expert on love, as well?' she said.

'Do I seem to be a know-all? I don't mean to. I only fell in love the once. It was a disaster and it nearly killed me. I thought that I would never lay myself open to that again. But I think perhaps I have, already.'

'You are in love?' she said.

'I might be. I don't know if such a thing as love exists. Perhaps it is only obsession. It has only occurred to me now that I might be in love. I might wake up tomorrow in another disaster. Do you know the essays of Francis Bacon?'

She said that she didn't know he wrote anything. She thought he was a painter.

He said he didn't know that Bacon was a painter at all.

The division of their knowledge silenced them for a few strides. When they spoke again, the atmosphere was broken. Perhaps they were each thinking too much.

When they were back at Ryme, Hugh refused her invitation to come into the big house. He said that he had work to be doing. But it was because he couldn't bear to meet Julius again. He went back to the South Cottage and changed into working clothes, and made his way cautiously to the Long Barn.

For the next few days he kept to his roof and waited for developments. He watched the comings and the goings of the house and heard the odd crash of object against wall. Sometimes he could talk to Evelyn or Hannah as they passed beneath the eaves of the Long Barn on their way to and from the horses with feed. Hannah went back to London at the end of the week. She said that she had to be at work but, even if she didn't, no one could have withstood the strain of that household for long.

On the Saturday morning, the day after Hannah went, it began to snow hard. Hugh watched it from his bed in the cottage for a while to see if it would melt or stay. It became a blizzard by mid-morning, reflecting a brilliant white light on the inside of the cottage. The white walls of the room took on a sterile glow. The air had become sharp rather than cold. He dressed with some enthusiasm and pulled a coat on and went to rescue some tools which he had left on the roof, and to make sure that everything would bear the weight of the snow.

While he was on the roof enjoying the snow, as you only can if you come from a country where it never snows properly, he heard the roar of a tractor in the yard below him, and he looked down into the white space that had been paved with damp bricks the day before. A tractor and trailer was crossing from the haybarn, the fall of the snow obliterating the tracks of it almost as soon as they were made.

Evelyn and another woman were walking across the yard in the wake of the tractor, like mourners after a hearse.

Evelyn had no coat on, and the woman walked beside her with an arm around her shoulder. There was something subdued, or funereal in their walking. The woman was comforting Evelyn in a hearty booming voice that was half-deadened in the falling snow. Evelyn, in response, was behaving in a suitably afflicted and grateful manner. The woman then called to her Labradors in a not dissimiliar voice. Hugh thought it looked as though something serious had happened. As though one of the horses had been killed.

He slid down a ladder and landed close to them. The woman was taking her leave of Evelyn, promising that, if there was anything she could do, she would, and Evelyn was thanking her. On Hugh's appearance, Evelyn briefly introduced them. It was Mrs Saville. Mrs Saville made to go, firmly embracing Evelyn and kissing her on both cheeks with astonishing tenderness for such a rough-hewn woman. Then she strode away, abusing her Labradors.

'Who was that?' said Hugh, now completely alarmed.

'The neighbour,' said Evelyn. 'She was bringing me some hay.'

'What's wrong? Are the horses all right?'

'Julius has left again,' she said, her eyes brimming as she did.

A wave of relief burst through him. Whether it was Julius's parting or the absence of a real disaster, he didn't know.

'Is that all?' he said, dismissively. He felt liberated by it. As if the place was theirs again. He said, 'How do you feel about it this time?'

She looked at him for a moment and then dropped her sorrowful act. 'Cross, actually,' she said. 'I wish the bugger would make up his mind.'

'Oh, good,' he said. He was pinning his arms by his sides so that they wouldn't rise and fold around her. He was trying not to smile too broadly at her disaster.

'That woman,' he said, thinking of something else to talk about, 'is she dykey?'

'Constance Saville? No.' She drew the no out to a long sound, more amused than shocked.

'She seems very fond of you,' he said.

'I think she is. She has the next biggest house in the village and

117

so she thinks that people like us should stick together. She is conscious of her position, having clawed her way up to it.'

'You don't like her?' he said.

Evelyn looked shocked that he might think so, and then guilty that she might have given him that impression. 'Oh dear,' she said, 'I am being unkind. I'm sure she is actually very fond of me. She has been terribly nice to me. I shouldn't say things like that.'

'If you ask me, she is terribly fond of you,' he said, mocking her voice as he said terribly.

They were still standing in the yard in the blizzard. Evelyn's hair was laced with the snow. He, with all his layers of clothing, began to feel cold and wet. He wondered at her not seeming to notice. The snow had covered Constance Saville's tracks, and drifted about their feet. Evelyn said that she didn't want to spoil the snow by walking on it. He said that he always did. He offered to carry her. He wanted to, but he said it as if it were a joke and that was how she took it. She led him back to her kitchen and her fishcakes, and they took up their lives as though Julius had never interrupted.

Although losing Julius in itself no longer bothered her, the disruption which it made in her life did. She still drank a lot and ate nothing. She had no idea what she was going to do. For now, her principal concern was that Vera Boldt should never live at Ryme.

THE ONLY REASON that Julius had had for returning was to see if he could persuade Evelyn to leave Ryme. He offered her money; he offered her a small flat in London. He reminded her that she had no right to be there. That Ryme was his and his alone. But these days Evelyn was beyond his bullying. Indeed, these days Julius's actions could no longer be described as bullying. He had weakened into a creature who was more likely to burst into tears than Evelyn was.

Evelyn sought the advice of a solicitor to know what her position was in law. She was told that she didn't have one. There was no marriage; no children in common. She had signed away her rights to the house. She would have no case in a courtroom. The best thing she could do was just to stay in the house for as long as she could bear it and, if she was offered a decent lump sum, to take it and clear out. 'And,' the solicitor said, 'whatever you do, don't weaken your position by compromising yourself.'

'What does that mean? How can I weaken a position I don't have?'

'Don't have any men in the house. You must only have women or couples even for the weekend. Don't start anything new until this is well over. He can try to evict you, but it will be more difficult for him if you can be seen to be blameless. I can't see that he will want a scandal.'

Evelyn knew what was meant. She contacted the publicity department of her publishers, and got them to send her the telephone numbers of all the tabloid newspapers. She got Hugh to drive her into Bruton where she bought chains and padlocks. Then she was ready. If Julius was going to evict her, then he was going to have to cut her free from the balustrade to which she would chain herself, with every gutter journalist in the country in attendance.

Fortified by this against the worst which the future could bring her, she settled down to being snowed-in with Hugh. She wasn't to know that he was in love with her. She was far too busy trying to keep herself out of love with him to see that his attitude to his thatching was not dissimilar to Penelope's attitude to her tapestry. She accepted the fact that he spent so much of his time in her company because he seemed to have so few friends in England and, even if he had, the snow limited any travel to see them. So there was a week of the two of them living in an unreal isolation, and each evening turning towards their own houses and their own beds.

By the thaw, Hugh Longford was at the end of his rope. He had no real idea why. It had never been his intention to declare his love to Evelyn. He was afraid that, if they had an affair, everything would be spoiled between them. He had no idea of what to do next. He had enough money to travel, and so he assumed that in the end he would have to finish the roof of the Long Barn and Ryme would be sold and he and Evelyn would part as friends. He could spend some time wandering across the world to forget her, as he had wandered here to forget the *hausfrau*.

And then there came a day when he got up in the morning and everything went wrong for him. You know what it is: the pipes burst and your toast burns and your car blows a gasket or whatever it is that cars blow; and even when you walk through the wood, you slip and land painfully on your arse, shredding a good pair of trousers. The more things go wrong, the worse your frame of mind is and the more likely it becomes that things will go wrong.

Hugh Longford decided to get drunk. He hadn't been drunk for a long time, but he could see that the only way out of the direction things were taking that day was by drastic action. He needed to shock his system. He went to the grocer's in Ryme Priory and bought two bottles of Scotch whisky and a packet of salted peanuts.

He sat for a long time in the South Cottage with his whisky before him on the table and a glass of it in his hand, but he had consumed no more than the salted peanuts, nor did he think he was likely to.

For two hours he sat, with the smell of whisky in his nostrils. He didn't want to drink it and he only had the vaguest idea why. It seemed ludicrous and petty to get drunk on his own, but he couldn't think of a likely companion. He thought about taking the train to Bristol and searching out Benedict, but really when he thought about it, he hardly knew Benedict at all. Their friendship, such as it was, had been conducted over cups of tea. And if he did go to Bristol, and he was in his cups, how would Benedict react when he confessed that he was in love with Benedict's mother?

It then seemed to him that there was some justice in Evelyn – as the source of his angst – becoming his friend in need. She was, after all, already a drinking companion. He had accompanied her in her drunkenness many times. It would not be strange if he asked her to accompany him in his. He gathered his armful of bottles and made for the big house.

'I need to get drunk,' he said to her. 'How about you?'

'You know me,' she said and went to get the glasses.

Perhaps you can see where all this is leading. It didn't necessarily seem so to them at the time. Let me illustrate:

Not far into the first bottle, Evelyn took out her cigarettes. Although she seldom smoked and he never did, she unconsciously offered him one.

'Why not?' he said. 'Cigarettes and whisky ...' He said it nonchalantly. It was meant as a joke. Something that would be meaningless in the atmosphere of trust between them. Perhaps it was a Freudian slip. Evelyn reacted as though it had been a direct assault on her honour.

'But not the wild women.' She said it sharply, reprovingly. She said it as though she was putting him firmly in his place and as though it would be pointless for him to try anything of that kind. He drew his horns in and kept quiet for a while. He wanted to say that it wasn't what he had meant at all, but sensed that it would only dig him in deeper.

Perhaps Evelyn was old and experienced enough to know what

was likely to happen. Perhaps, in the moment she said that, she was defending herself against the compromise that her solicitor had warned her about. She was simply stating her case, just in case.

It was all forgotten by the end of the first bottle. They had baked potatoes for supper. He scraped the insides out and coloured them, blue and yellow and pink and green, and put them back again. They played scrabble and they both cheated. As the fire dimmed and they were both too drunk to fetch more wood, so they moved closer towards it, splayed across the floor either side of the scrabble board. By the end of the whisky their heads were practically in the chimney. He kissed her. It seemed the only thing to do. They were both drunk enough to have forgotten any reason they might have had for not kissing before.

She tried to focus on him with her golden eyes, but he was too close and so, not knowing in her modesty what he might say to her, she said to him. 'I'm going to bed. You can come too, if you like. But you don't have to. I don't mind.'

He said, 'Neither do I.'

He followed her upstairs. I don't think you need to know much more, except that everything was bliss for them, and neither of them had ever encountered anyone who had made them as happy before. The whisky was neither here nor there. Whisky could get in the way of sex, I suppose. But, if what you are consummating has anything to do with love, then whisky will never stop you.

So, in that night they underwent that transformation from a half life to a complete one. It wasn't necessary any more to go from lover to friend to lover, getting a scrap of what you needed from each person, and always feeling that there was something missing. Life wasn't going to be perfect for them, but they would get closer to happiness than most people ever do.

HE WAS THE first to wake in the morning, and he waited without moving for her to open her eyes. He had a romantic notion that he would like to see her yellow irises reflect the sunlight. When she woke she tried to hide her face from him. 'What's wrong?' he said. She said she had no make-up on. 'I hate make-up,' he said. 'I want to see you.' She told him not to be a beast, but he caught her and pulled her face around, and although she hid the most of it with her hair, he could see her eyes, and he saw that they were a pale shade of grey. Not yellow at all.

He thought he might still be asleep, might still be drunk or dreaming, and he thought in a surreal way that he was responsible for the colour that was missing from her eyes. That she had lost it through his fucking her. It seemed to tie in with how he had always felt about sex and, for a moment, his memory of the night before was marred by the thought that he had taken something from her, just as he had always imagined he had taken something from everyone else. It had seemed at the time that no one was robbing anyone. He had thought, in his movement, from the way they were doing it, that he was doing it for the first time. But now her eyes were colourless.

'Oh fuck,' he said, 'what's wrong with your eyes?'

She was alarmed by his voice, which was close to tears, although she couldn't see his face properly until she had her lenses in.

'I haven't got my lenses in,' she said. Her voice told she was hurt by his disappointment in her. She felt he would never forgive her for being only herself. This was her experience of men.

For all she knew, Hugh Longford was no longer a friend to her. He had become a lover, and stated his side of the sexual divide. There was no reason why he shouldn't behave as men were cursed to. But he didn't. Instead of feeling cheated by her, he laughed and said how wonderful it was, and he asked her if he could try her yellow lenses on.

'What do you mean?' she said. 'How can it be wonderful to have grey eyes?'

'I have grey eyes,' he said.

She looked at him. She squinted to see him, although she was only inches away.

'Can't you see anything?' he said.

'It isn't all vanity, you know.' She was holding her hair across her face again, more from the motivation of a leper than a dancer. 'I am blind as a bat. I need yellow light or I would be blinder. Are your eyes grey? Really?'

'Haven't you noticed? I thought the first thing that a novelist noticed was the colour of our eyes. My eyes, if you want to know, are an enchanting shade of slate-grey. Put that in your books and smoke it.'

'I suppose,' she said, 'it's the difference between fiction and life. Eyes are the first thing they tell you about in a book and the last thing you notice in a person. I never notice eyes. Perhaps it is because I haven't been able to see them for so much of my life.'

He could feel a brittleness in the way she spoke. A coolness in her manner that contrasted with the warmth of her skin. He thought perhaps that she had had this conversation with more than one person in the past, in the same circumstances, possibly in the same bed.

He felt slightly uncouth, as though his morning-after manners weren't quite up to hers. He could feel that she had had years more practice at this level of morality, in this sinless atmosphere, in this Godless nation.

Rather than despise her for all this, he admired her, as the possessor of a talent he had yet to acquire. He wondered, at that moment, if a woman of her morality, of her guiltless sensuality, would be capable of love. If she would ever love him, or if it was best not to mention it.

They had a day of it that day. Unless you are very young, or cold, you must know what it is like. You must have had the swarming happiness of a first reciprocation and a lightness to your walking and the smile of an idiot across your face.

They had awoken in a bedroom that still bore the traces of Julius's residence, and so, as soon as they had bidden each other good morning in the manner they had said good night, Hugh Longford went prowling through the house, looking for a fresh earth for them to settle in. As soon as he had decided on the best room, he went back to fetch Evelyn and to tell her she was moving.

It was a large, high-ceilinged room, with windows that looked out over the sunken rose garden and the lawns and yews. Out to the left there were orchards and the tulip tree; to the right, among the woods, there was a glimpse of the South Cottage.

He said, 'This is perfect. We can see the winter aconites from our bed. There will be apple blossom at Easter and the smell of the roses will come up to us in June.'

She said, 'But we can't have this room. This is the room that Sarah Bliss stays in.'

'Sarah Bliss can stay somewhere else,' he said, as he left the room. She stayed by the window and saw him reappear in the garden. He was barefoot, and wearing an old silk kimono of hers that flapped around his bare calves as he crossed the frosted grass below her. He went through the hedges and she stayed by the window, waiting to see what he did.

He brought a branch of Chinese witchhazel and put it by the bed. She was cross with him for plundering the garden, but he made her smell the yellow ribbons and she forgave him, although she could not lose her foreboding that, once he was a lover, Hugh Longford would be no different from any man she had ever known.

Her agent called her, late in the morning, saying had she forgotten that she was supposed to be in London. She seized the chance to get away. It wasn't that she didn't enjoy his seduction, but that the overwhelming extent to which she did enjoy it frightened her.

He mended his car and drove her to the station. He would have come with her but she didn't suggest it. He came back to Ryme on his own, determined to finish the roof before she got back. He could sense her anxiety, and wanted to be able to get out of the way if it turned out that he wasn't wanted. For all he knew, she had regretted the whole affair already. For all he knew at that stage, she never slept with anyone more than once. From his post-coital euphoria of the morning he had descended into a jilted depression by dusk.

She was staying with Sarah Bliss in London. She had left him the telephone number. She said it was in case anything happened. Afterwards, he had no idea what this could mean, whether she was expecting a calamity, or whether she meant him to phone her anyway. Four times that evening, as he sat in the South Cottage, he decided to phone her and went to the big house. By the time he was standing by the phone he would think the better of it. Once he dialled, but the number was engaged. Each time he went back to the South Cottage.

The South Cottage didn't seem like a home to him any longer. He knew that, no matter what happened, he would have to leave it soon. It seemed cold and he couldn't settle in it. He could hardly bear to turn the lights or heaters on. He sat in his coat, before the meaningless flickering of the television, more often watching the patterns it threw on the walls than anything drawn on the screen.

He mulled and thought and brooded over it. In his lowest moments, he accused her of calling young men to her bed every day of the week; of having a stable of well-designed lovers in London. She would probably never want to speak to him again; she might stay in London until he had gone away.

These phantom lovers he gave her tortured him for the evening. He began to resign himself to losing her, and began to stem whatever it was in him that was like regret. He denied that he ever was in love or that love was possible. He thought about a move to Normandy, or sliding across the surface of the world like an Australian. He thought about his life and decided that it wasn't enough for him. He had gone as far as thatching was likely to take him.

He felt one hand with the thumb of another, and knew the difference between this thatcher's hand and a normal hand. He had seen the hands of old thatchers and they were his nightmare, and he knew, unless he stopped now, he would soon be an old thatcher. At the end of his life, if someone asked him what he had done with it, the answer he would have to give if he was still a thatcher would be the same as the answer he would give now. The next forty years stretched before him as a repetitive waste.

He tried hard to make the connection between his dissatisfaction with thatching and his obsession with Evelyn. He had a premonition that Evelyn could be the catalyst if he were to try to change himself. His ambitions were still amorphous, but he knew that there was something within him that he had yet to express.

He sat all that night in the cold and the dark, alternately loving Evelyn and practising indifference to her, in case she mightn't love him.

In London, Evelyn's mind was no easier but, at least, she had Sarah Bliss to talk to. She said, 'I've done a terrible thing. I've slept with the thatcher.'

Sarah said, 'Why is that terrible? Does he smell?'

'No,' she said, 'he isn't that sort of thatcher. It is terrible because he is very young.'

Sarah said, 'I hope you aren't going to fall in love with him.'

'No,' said Evelyn, 'I'm hardly going to do that.' It was as soon as she said this that she realised she was probably already in love.

She knew that, if she admitted this to Sarah or anyone else, there might be a lecture. She knew that, if it was terrible and unfair to sleep with someone as much her junior as Hugh Longford was, then it was a lot worse to be in love with him. She thought that the last thing he probably wanted was a middle-aged woman cluttering up his life, just as the last thing she probably needed was a young man complicating hers – and exhausting her with his youth.

By half-past four in the morning, he was no further on in his resolution. He was still in his coat in the same chair. Two glowing bars of a heater had taken the place of the television before him. He was drinking some Bulgarian claret in an effort to induce sleepiness, but still he wasn't finished with turning Evelyn over in his mind. He hadn't secured her a place in any scheme he could think of. And still he thought that she might come back from London and cut him dead, recovered from a drunken slip of her guard, and back on her chatelaine pedestal. He knew that, from her point of view, or from anyone else's, she was too old for him and too famous and too set in her society. That the easiest thing would be to finish the roof, collect the money from Julius, and slip away to set it all behind him as a slice of life. A small exercise in his basic training.

He could be finished with the Long Barn that day, if he set to it. He could get away from Ryme before he was forced away. He decided to go and look at the roof and see exactly how it was. He could look at it by the headlights of his car.

The morning was as cold as a midwinter morning can get at five o' clock or just before it. It was a miracle that the car started. The ground everywhere was solid with ice and you felt that, if you shouted, the trees would crack and fall apart with the sound of your voice. He parked his car in the middle of the yard, with the engine running and the headlights blaring at the barn.

As he shuffled about on top of the roof at seven below zero, not really at all sure why he was up there, because he knew already the exact state of everything from the afternoon before, he thought, all of a sudden, that he was being very stupid and these were precisely the conditions that could give him a fall from the roof, and what good or use could he be to himself or anyone else then? The ladders were coated in ice and his hands were so numb that he couldn't open or close his fingers, and in spite of the headlights he could see almost nothing. He told himself that he must be drunk to have gone up there in the first place, but he knew it would take more than the one bottle of dreadful wine to make him drunk or stupid in this cold.

Perhaps he was in too much of a hurry to get down, once he had realised the precariousness of his position. Perhaps he willed what happened next because it was a way to jolt himself out of one set of circumstances and into another, achieving the same general effect as his drunkenness two nights before. Perhaps it was the ghosts of Ryme that pushed him off the roof, since it was their purpose that was served in the end. Whatever it was, he went sliding from the ladders and shot over the eaves. His fall was partly broken by an iron rod that was facing upwards, which shot up the inside of his trouser leg, luckily, on the outer side, scraping the flesh off his thigh and hip. As he fell, in that odd way which one does, he was thinking that this might all be for the better, and a small injury would keep him at Ryme long enough for Evelyn to fall in love with him. He could hear his own deep shout of fear and agony (quite an impressive, angry sort of noise, he thought at the time), and he

128

could feel the iron scraping past his leg and hear the ripping of his jeans. Then he hit the ice-hard ground with a crack, and he sat there, cursing and swearing at his own stupidity.

His first reaction was to get in the car and drive back to the cottage to change. He accomplished this without any trouble, unaware that he had anything more than a scratch on his leg.

There was a stiffness in his foot as he pressed it against the accelerator, but it wasn't what you could call a pain. It wasn't until he stood in the light of the South Cottage kitchen that he realised there was any seriousness to his injury. There was a trail of blood from the door to where he stood and a pool of blood about his feet. He began to pull his boots off, and it was then he realised that his right foot might be broken. Slowly, he removed the sock. The pain was excruciating, now that the boot no longer held his foot together. He placed his foot on the chair opposite him and sat for a while gazing at it, considering what he might do next.

He could probably have driven himself to a hospital, but he had no idea where the nearest hospital was. He decided to drive himself to the big house instead and use the telephone there, if only to find out how to get himself into a casualty unit. He began to move across the kitchen, holding up his right leg like an injured dog. The tear along his leg, now that it had begun to dry out, sent a wrenching pain through him with every movement. He managed to drive by using his left foot on the accelerator. It took a long time to turn the car around, but he was grateful to have something other than his pain to concentrate on.

He found that, in his agony, his mind had acquired an unreal lucidity. He found himself attending to details, like closing doors after himself and hopping across the hall on the wooden parts and not the carpets, so as not to stain them with blood. He went to Evelyn's office and sat by her telephone. There was a clock before him. It was not yet half-past five.

He thought it was a pity that it wasn't a more civilised hour. If it had been eight o' clock he could have phoned Evelyn to tell her about it. The way things were, he might have to stay in hospital, and never have a chance to speak to her again. He desperately wanted to speak to her. He wondered if he could put up with the pain until eight, and phone her first. To telephone Evelyn was the only thing he really wanted to do.

The time passed, some of it awash with pain, so that once or twice he began to feel heady as though he might faint. But most of the time he simply watched the movement of the hands on the clock, keeping himself completely still because of the pain, that shot through him with every movement of his own.

At five minutes to eight Evelyn woke up in Sarah Bliss's spare room. She got out of her bed and went downstairs. There was no one else awake in the house. As she passed the telephone, it rang. She picked the receiver up before the first ring had finished. Hugh asked if Evelyn was there.

'It's me,' she said.

'It's me,' he replied.

'I know,' she said. 'I was wondering when you would ring.'

They talked about one thing and another before he casually mentioned that he thought he might have broken his foot. He said it as though he was embarrassed by it. He could hear himself being the brave little soldier. She showed all the concern and sympathy and alarm that he could ever have hoped for. She told him he was mad for not going straight to hospital. He belittled it and said that he wasn't going to bleed to death.

At that moment, he might have bled to death and not noticed. As he spoke to her he felt no pain at all and forgot his discomfort. He wanted to talk about other things, but she made him promise to get himself to hospital as quickly as he could. She made him promise not to drive, but to get an ambulance or, at the very least, a taxi. She insisted that she would come back on the first train possible.

At the hospital, he found himself feeling more and more sheepish each time he had to explain his accident. For a thatcher to fall from a roof seemed more like professional incompetence than falling prey to an occupational hazard. It was probably because of this that he fought with the nurses. He probably had to restore his self-esteem somehow.

He was wearing a pair of voluminous white linen trousers. The sort you wear in summer. They were his favourite trousers, but he had thought that they would be the most sensible thing to wear for the journey into hospital. A bit of blood would wash out, after all. The nurses, scissor-happy as nurses always are, were about to set about cutting them off him. He yelled at them to stop. They said it was the only way to get them off and he said it was nonsense, and everyone slightly lost their temper until the nurses walked off in a huff and said he could get his own trousers off and see if they cared. With a lot of pain and manœuvring, he managed to remove them, but it took as much charm as he could muster to get the right side of the nurses again.

So it was the middle of the afternoon by the time he got back to Ryme again. Evelyn was already there. She came out at the sound of the taxi and brought him into the kitchen of the big house, fussing in case his crutches should slip on the flagstones.

'Crutches are nothing,' he said. 'I am used to crutches.' Once again he heard the brave soldier in his voice and wished that he had said something else.

'Are you hungry?' she said. 'What would you like? I don't think there is anything except fishcakes. What did they say at the hospital?'

'Fishcakes are fine,' he said. 'We could go to the pub. Do you know they tried to cut my trousers off? I don't know what I would have come home in. My best trousers. It seemed a bit much to ruin three pairs of trousers in one week.'

He knew he was being odd; behaving as though he was lightheaded, but there was nothing he could do about it. He felt awkward standing before her in this incapacitated state. He felt as though he had been in some sense neutered and made harmless. He was used to it being the other way around, with him in control and her needing the help. He blathered on while she fetched the fishcakes.

'What is actually wrong with you?' she asked, in a voice that cut through his.

'It's nothing,' he said. 'I've broken a tiny bone somewhere, and lost a lot of skin. They said I'll be fine in three weeks. I'm just supposed to keep my leg higher than my waist as much as possible. It's all the usual stuff.'

'You had better move into a room here,' she said. 'I'm not running backwards and forwards to the South Cottage all day.'

'That's fine,' he said. 'It's kind, but I can easily look after myself. Or if I can't I can go and stay with the Kopses or go back to Ireland.'

They watched each other's faces, each searching for clues as to how the other one really felt. It was like a staring match. One of them had to give in first.

'No,' she said. 'You had better stay here.' She turned away as she said this, as though she had been defeated. She was back at her old stance at the Aga, pushing fishcakes around the pan, with her hair held over the bottom half of her face. He had expected her to be either warmer or cooler towards him. He hadn't expected her to seem to feel exactly as he did. He hadn't expected this equality. He thought it was time that he capitulated as well.

'All right,' he said. 'But only if we can move into that east room.'

Still clutching her hair across her mouth and nose, and without turning towards him, she muttered so that he could barely hear it, 'I suppose I had better go and make up the bed then.'

She left the fishcakes; left the room, going out of the door nearest to her so that she didn't have to pass by him or look at him. She left him stupefied to some degree.

When he heard her footfalls over his head, he struggled to his feet. He didn't know what he was going to say to her, or that he was going to say anything to her. He still had no real idea what was going to happen.

It took him a long time to climb the stairs, with one leg and a crutch. He could see that these stairs were going to be his worst problem. He had time, as he went up them step by step, to look at all the carving properly, and to notice the colouring of the stone. At this new pace of his, the whole house seemed quite different. Slowed down, he was forced to look at it at the pace it was meant for. He moved slowly towards the east room, where Evelyn was throwing white sheets out over the bed, with her back to him as though she hadn't heard him coming. He swung to a half halt beside her, and touched her on the elbow.

That was, I think, the real beginning of the affair. Each one of them was sure that they were in love with the other one, although no one was admitting anything yet. When they did it that day, they no longer felt as though they were on trial; as though they were doing it with a stranger. They became unselfconscious. They could talk in the middle. She couldn't remember life ever having been like that before. He was sure it had never been so.

Afterwards, they lay in the scent of the witchhazel that was still by the bed where he had left it. The gas heater spat in the middle of the room, and her head was locked in his elbow. He couldn't see her face, but he assumed that she was as contented as himself. He had no idea that, while all he could see was the beginning and how wonderful it was all going to be, she could see nothing but the end and the awfulness and the fact that their affair was hopeless from the start. That he was bound to leave her, and the sooner he did it the less painful it would be for her.

She decided to leave things as they were until his leg was better but to hold herself back. The house was sure to be sold by the summer. She had no idea what she would do after Ryme. Sarah Bliss wanted her to move in with her in London, but she couldn't see that far ahead. If she could see a future, she couldn't see that Hugh had any part in it, that he would want her once he was mobile and fit again.

FOR A WEEK or so, they were left completely to themselves. They saw no one except Mrs Charles who came to clean the house in the mornings. Mrs Charles approved of Hugh, because she could see that Evelyn was so much more cheerful. Her behaviour towards him was gruff and disapproving because she thought that someone had to keep him in his place, to remind him that his only function in life was to be a comfort to Evelyn. After two years of cleaning her house, it was Mrs Charles's chief ambition that Evelyn should find happiness. She saw Hugh, not as the man who would take care of Evelyn's future, but as a cheerful interregnum who would do for her while things were being sorted out. It was a logical way to look at it, and a point of view which Evelyn herself found easiest to adopt. It was only Hugh Longford, at this stage, who could see any future at all, and this he kept to himself because he knew how hollow promises of eternity could sound in the early stages of a connection.

The weather was cold and fine. It was early February, but the date had no meaning to him. When he thought about every other February in Ireland, he had no memory of this January weather. The Februarys he remembered were mild and soft with warm rain from the Atlantic; a false spring before the blastings of March. This suspension of weather gave him a sense of unreality. The year seemed to have stood still since he had moved into the east room, as if Ryme was under the spell of the Snow Queen. The brittle weather stayed with them as long as he was on his crutches. For as long as he was powerless.

They were happy for this first half of February. They didn't know each other well enough for conflict. Perhaps that is what a honeymoon period is. Julius seemed to have disappeared from the face of the earth. Once, Hugh wondered aloud what had happened to Julius. 'Perhaps he is dead?' he said.

Evelyn said, 'I should be so lucky.'

'You wouldn't be saying that if he owed you money,' he said. She smiled at him, as if that was the end of it, as if these weeks were not to be ruined by talking about Julius, dead or alive. The subject fell away from them.

Once, she asked him what he would do when his leg was better. He wanted to answer that he would stay with her, but the tone in which she had asked him implied that he wouldn't stay. If he wanted to stay, he would have to ask her if he might. He was no more prepared to do this and be refused or, what was worse, allowed to stay on sufferance, than she was prepared to ask him if he would stay.

'I don't know,' he said. 'I've been offered some work in Normandy. But I don't know if I want to be a thatcher for the rest of my life.'

'Normandy, how wonderful,' she said.

'You could come too,' he said, 'if you like. But you don't have to. I don't mind.'

'I have to stay here,' was all she said. She could have no conception of herself as belonging to his baggage train. She thought he might only be offering out of politeness. She was still afraid of what might happen if she was no longer in control. If it wasn't her house and her fishcakes and if he wasn't tied down with crutches. And what would he be doing with her, in any case? He should marry someone more like Hannah and have children – and be happy.

This winter honeymoon ended on St Valentine's Day. David Magna decided to throw a St Valentine's massacre. (Do you remember him? He is the small silent one who is married to Emir, Sarah Bliss's best friend.) Evelyn decided to give a dinner before it. She had been promised by Emir Magna that Vera Boldt was not to be invited. She was encouraged by Emir to bring her young man out into society and herself with him. Emir, being firmly planted in her own circumstances, was a great one for moving everyone else on to better things.

Benedict came down from Bristol and the Bennets came and the Kopses. The supper that Evelyn gave them was so awful that they were all charmed by it. It was a sort of dreadful pasta followed by apple pudding. Evelyn ate nothing and was unaware of how terrible her food was. Because she used to cook well in the past, she assumed that she still did. Hugh made some remark about them all being poisoned before the massacre, but no one seemed to understand it, except Benedict, who looked offended on behalf of his mother. At the other end of the table, Hilda Bennet was asking Susan Kopse what she thought of Evelyn's Irish lord.

'Hugh?' said Susan Kopse. 'Do you mean Hugh? Hugh isn't a lord.'

'Oh, but he must be,' Hilda shrieked. 'Ned has been telling everyone that he is.'

'I only said that he might be.' Ned glared at Hilda as though he thought she had destroyed the subtlety of his joke. Ned had the most wonderful costume of anyone. He was dressed exactly as a gangster, even with a floor-length bearskin coat. Hilda, for reasons only known to herself, was dressed as a schoolgirl. She always dressed as a schoolgirl for these things, no matter what the theme for the costumes was. People had ceased to comment on it years ago. Now, she shook out her pigtails and tried to seem indifferent to Ned's disapproval. Benedict, who sat on her other side, said nothing. He had suspected that there was something going on, and now he knew what it was. He spent the rest of the supper glaring at Hugh, who was too busy gazing at Evelyn to notice. When they travelled to the massacre, Benedict made sure that he was in the other car. He was too angry, just at that moment, to trust himself in close proximity to them.

The cars had to be parked a long way from the party, and there was a quarter of a mile of frosted road for them to walk. Benedict found that Hugh was swinging along beside him on his crutches, in a companionable sort of way. Benedict was dressed as a Chicago newsboy, with a cap askew on his head. The effect was to make him look positively thuggish. The sulking projection of his lower lip increased the effect. If Hugh could have seen him, he might have kept his distance, but Hugh was busy trying to make out the road in front of him. He had no imagination for costumes, and had just put on an old dinner jacket to come as a speakeasy client with his hair oiled down. He was slightly puzzled, though not wholly surprised by Benedict's silence. On the one hand he knew how he himself would feel if one of his friends moved in with his mother. On the other hand, Benedict was one of the heathen liberal English, a race, he had always understood, which would condone sexual aberrations.

While they went along, and Hugh became more aware of Benedict's taciturnity, he tried to think of something innocuous to say. They passed a gate, and Benedict, suddenly and with one movement, put his hand out and swung himself over it. It could have been that he was going to pee, but there was something too explosive and violent in his movement. Hugh, in his momentum, carried on. What could he do? He was in no state to swing over a gate.

Benedict pissed as if he was trying to poison the ground beneath him. He was furious with his mother. From his point of view, Hugh hardly came into it at all. Hugh was so obviously a pawn in his mother's charm. If he blamed Hugh for anything, it was for his stupidity in allowing himself to be seduced into this disastrous liaison. Why couldn't Evelyn have been happy to stay with Julius? Julius had always been good to her; had taken them in for no advantage of his own; had been a father to him. Julius had been happy to stay with her for all those years that she had been a wife to him. It wasn't Julius who was to blame if Evelyn had begun to ignore him. If she had begun to fight with him and ceased to charm him. He wasn't at fault if Vera Boldt had swept Julius off his feet when he was being badly treated at home. Benedict blamed his mother for the entire crisis. That had been fine as long as she was suffering for it, but here she was in possession of Ryme and Hugh Longford (hobbled, it seemed, for her convenience), while Julius was roaming the country and living out of a suitcase. Julius had turned up at his digs in Bristol the other week. He was in tears, quite inconsolable. The whole thing had been a terrible embarrassment. What do you do with a weeping man in his fifties? One who is a victim of women, no less than yourself? When Benedict finished, he stood in the road again, putting off his entrance to the party. He couldn't be responsible for what he might say to the first woman he met.

Ned Bennet was hurrying towards him. He had been as far as the door; had looked at the scene within in complete horror and was now retreating. He came up abreast of where Benedict was standing.

'I'm not going in there,' he said.

'Me neither,' said Benedict. They sloped off together, each happy to have found someone as bad-tempered as themselves.

You don't really want to know about that party, do you? I find parties rather sad. Especially those ones where everyone exposes themselves by dressing up. All those men, like Paul Boldt, who leap at the chance to get into women's clothes, and poor Hilda Bennet, abandoned in her schoolgirl garb. She sat in a corner (the most prominent corner she could find) for the evening, discreetly complaining of her ill-use when anyone came her way. David Magna, who stood about in a white tie and tails, believing that he had nothing more to do as a host than be as handsome as he believed he was. He couldn't bear to open his mouth in case it should disarrange his face. He greeted his guests with a slow pompous nod and a wave of his long cigarette holder. Emir Magna balanced this up nicely by being completely soused and determined to enjoy herself. She and Sarah Bliss, who was in a similar condition to her, wove their way about the room, arm in arm, falling into the laps of their friends and spreading scandal. Two jazz bands played at either end of the room and middle-aged artists did tame impressions of the charleston.

The worst moment was perhaps when Paul Boldt came up to Evelyn and Hugh, and began to talk in a loud voice about how grateful he was to Julius for relieving him of Vera. It mightn't have been so bad if he hadn't been wearing a gold shimmy dress and a cloche hat, all sixteen stones of him. Emir and Sarah followed closely in his wake, saying hadn't they heard, Paul Boldt had bought a sheepdog to replace Vera, and wasn't going to have her back this time.

From where he sat Hugh saw quite a lot of Emir and Sarah, swooping down on him from the darkness as they wobbled about the room. Otherwise, it was not a comfortable evening for him.

People would keep thinking that his bandaged foot was some sort of costume, and kick it just to be sure.

In the morning, Hugh seriously thought that Benedict was going to hit him. He made sure that everywhere he stood, he had something soft behind him to fall on, and convinced himself that being hit for Evelyn was, all in all, a small price.

But Benedict never came that close. He got in his taxi and left as soon as he could, and without actually addressing a word to Hugh.

As he went, Evelyn said, 'Oh dear. It is so embarrassing. That baby boy has such dreadful manners. He is beginning to be like his father.' She said it in a stagy, dismissive voice, as if Benedict was more than she could think about.

'It's my fault,' Hugh said, as a statement of fact rather than an apology.

Evelyn said, 'Oh no. It is nothing to do with you. I know what Benedict is like. He will just have to sort himself out. You mustn't worry about it.'

Emir Magna and Sarah Bliss came to tea that afternoon. Emir brought her five shy girls and Sarah brought some gin. Hugh was the only man among eight women, and they treated him as a novice one of themselves, so that he felt like a eunuch in a harem.

Sarah Bliss had just jettisoned her last man and decided on her next one. She had a grim, faraway look about her, because she hadn't yet secured the new man. She had to be careful with this one, she had decided, because he was to be a permanent fixture. She was too preoccupied to talk to Emir or to Evelyn properly, and so she stood by the window most of the time, watching the horses. She had a sort of graceful awkwardness about her like, do you know, one of those very superior foals; large-kneed and self-possessed.

Emir Magna was the odd one out. She was still in the thrall of the same rather unsatisfactory man, one that she had had for twenty years. Although no one thought he looked very bright (that vain and vacant way he would stare at you for minutes without blinking), he was expert at psychological warfare. He had kept a strong character like Emir depressed and where he wanted her for half of her life.

Evelyn stretched across the tea tray on the floor and poured their tea and tried to make conversation with the girls. They all blinked back with their father's vacant eyes. She passed a cup to Emir who said, 'Evelyn! God! What happened to your finger?'

'I broke it on Julius's nose,' she said.

'Did you?' said Emir. 'Did it work? What effect did it have on him?'

'Well, of course, it didn't work,' said Hugh. 'He ran off with old Snagglenickers, didn't he?'

'I would have thought you should be grateful for that,' said Sarah.

'Gratitude isn't one of my faults,' he said.

'I beat David up once,' said Emir. 'It was absolutely useless. He just said that it was a symbolic castration and he could never do it with me again. And he hasn't.'

Hugh winced with embarrassment. He thought that Emir must have forgotten the children were there. But the girls carried on nibbling their scones as if they heard it every day.

'Did you beat him up badly?' Evelyn asked her casually.

'Dreadfully,' said Emir, making a face. 'You know what a wimp he is. I had to stop because his shrieking upset the poultry. They wouldn't lay for weeks. It's a good thing my baby girls weren't there.'

Her baby girls all preserved their attitudes. It was true they were used to this, but they still writhed with shame inside themselves. Only Hugh, who came from a less liberal society, could see this. Suddenly, one of the girls asked if they could play outside, and they all vanished with handfuls of biscuit.

The talk carried on. Hugh had nothing to say in it. At times he felt he was being allowed to listen by dispensation; other times he felt that everything was being said for his benefit. That in subtle ways he was being warned of his duties as consort to Evelyn; that the three women were ganging up on him in his incapacitated state. Outside, the girls skated on the ice of the fountain, or pressed their faces close to it to see the fish below. They had lost their shyness and sullenness, and they shrieked and ran, watched by Sarah Bliss's gaunt profile by the window.

Sarah Bliss said, 'What will happen? Who will get all this? I suppose it will be sold.'

'I expect so,' said Evelyn.

'Will you get half?'

'No, nothing. I have no rights in this. It all belongs to Julius. If I could, I don't think I would keep it. I always thought it was immoral that the two of us should rattle around in a house this size while Hannah has nowhere to live in London.'

'What happens if Julius dies?' Emir asked this in a voice that was suddenly sharp. 'Who inherits?'

'Me, actually,' said Evelyn. 'We have mutually beneficial wills. I can't remember why. There was a reason. Why? Is that likely? Do you think that Snagglenickers will poison him?'

'I heard a rumour that Paul was going to kill him,' said Emir. 'But these days Paul just seems terribly pleased to have Vera off his hands. Perhaps Hugh would kill Julius for you. He looks the sort that might do it.'

'Thanks,' said Hugh.

'And now he is blushing,' said Emir. 'Aren't young men sweet?'

'I don't know,' said Evelyn. 'I can't bear the idea of Julius's avenging ghost bleating after me everywhere I go.'

'Are you working?' Sarah Bliss interjected from the window.

'No,' said Evelyn, ashamed of herself. 'I am supposed to be. Perhaps this is all for the best. Perhaps I will have to move back to London and start working again and have a whole new life.'

'I can't see that there is much thatching to be done in London,' Emir said. She was batting her eyelids at Hugh. He still hadn't decided whether to be charmed or irritated by her.

'Not a whole lot, no,' he said.

'Hugh is going to Normandy,' Evelyn said.

'Oh,' said both of the other women.

That left them all with such a hump in the conversation that they had to go out into the garden to get over it. They needed to talk about *Iris histrioides* and the division of snowdrops. Hugh swung about among them on his crutches like a bell, while the children joined themselves head to feet and rolled down the banks of the croquet lawn in one long sausage. Someone took photographs of that day, and so it was all long remembered, remembered with the clarity which only an artificial image can give you.

After they had all left, Evelyn seemed sullen to Hugh. It was more than he could bear and he goaded her and poked at her until

141

she lost her temper and accused him of what she thought was the matter.

'If you want to go and have an affair with Sarah Bliss, you can,' she said.

'What do you mean? Why would I want to have an affair with Sarah Bliss? Why would she want one with me?'

'Oh, come on,' she said. 'You can't pretend that you weren't bending over backwards to flirt with her. I know Sarah. She is without a man. You would do nicely. You are perfectly free to go and live with her if you want.'

'I don't believe this,' he said. 'In the first place I don't need you to tell me what I am free to do. If I wanted to go and live with someone else I don't need your permission. In the second place I am not going to be deliberately rude to every single female that I meet just for the sake of your peace of mind. And even at that, I barely spoke a word to Sarah Bliss all afternoon. If I was flirting with anyone it was with Emir. And, just because your last husband was a rat, there is no need to behave as though I might be the same.'

'I would just like you to tell me,' she said. 'If you are leaving I would just like some warning. I know that this is finite, and that you will leave, but I would just like some warning.'

They said nothing for a while which gave him time to be amused by her jealousy, and to see the reasoning behind her insecurity. She had been betrayed by one friend, and now she must watch all of her friends for a while. He could say nothing. He could make no promises because it would be only playing a game and indulging her insecurity. He had decided not to lie to her.

He led her upstairs for her answer and, afterwards, on their bed, he said to her, 'Well, this is no good. I can't leave you to live out the rest of your life on Victoria Station. What are we to do?'

'What are you going to do about it? Murder Julius?'

'I might,' he said. 'It seems I had better do whatever is necessary. Whatever it will take. It seems it is time that we began to think about what to do for the rest of our lives.'

'If only you could get away with it,' she said. It was still a joke to her. She was two sentences behind him.

He looked at her quite seriously, and said, 'I will, if you want me to.'

There was nothing she could say to this. To continue with the joke might only encourage him. To fall into seriousness would only give the whole idea a credibility which frightened her. He had turned away from her now, and was pouring juice into a glass for her. Watching the back of his long neck and the feminine slope of his shoulders, she wondered if it was possible that he would murder for her.

There was a time when he had brought a dead hare to her cats, and had expected her gratitude, or at least her collusion. He had baited them with it by the back door, shaking it in front of them to heat their blood and make them play with it. He had called to her to come and watch and witness how her tame beloveds were growling and tearing at the corpse. She cowered in the kitchen, waiting for the blooding to be over, and for her cats to resume their domestic pretences. When he joined her, there was blood on his hands and a look of exaltation on his face. She wondered now if he would get the same thrill from Julius's blood. She could see his magenta thatcher's hands closing around Julius's thin neck, and Julius's lashless eyes batting like the eyes of a dying chicken.

It was only for a moment that she imagined a death would solve anything. She knew, in fact, that death is too much of a catalyst to be a solution. If you push the pendulum out that far then you must always be waiting for the return.

Her moment was past when he looked at her again, still all seriousness, and she realised that he would do anything for her. She wondered if that was love or blindness, and she preferred to think it was love. She decided that he loved her. For the first time in a long time, she abandoned all her cynicism and all her education. She allowed herself to be suffused by that heady emotional romanticism, the existence of which she had always disclaimed. She allowed him, bloodstained hands and all, to assume heroic proportions. It occurred to her, on the road to this estimation, that he was only being gallant. He was only saying the brave things to her that a woman would expect in bed. He was only gazing at her in adoration because it was a tactic of lovemaking. But then she curled herself around him and put her thigh across the flat of his stomach and buried her fist deep in his armpit and her face in his clavicle and, feeling as though she had been made drunk by proximity to him and wasn't responsible for what she might say, she said, 'I love you.'

It was quite a shock to them both. Things, up until now, had been so civilised. There had been no occasion so far for this pure love to be spattered with the mud of emotional complication. Hugh Longford stopped the hand that was stroking her and, as if he had suddenly realised how uncomfortable he was, he said, 'Hang on, you are hurting my foot. Just move for a minute.'

She moved and he moved, and all their intimacy was broken and they were only two naked people on the same bed. He knew he could have saved it all by declaring his love in return, but he had repelled the instinctive I love you, too, that had leapt into his throat. That was too glib. That was only a reaction and not an action of his own. He felt that his declaration should wait for its own moment and not be trailing out in the wake of hers. Besides, he had always intended to be the first to declare and resented her usurpation.

All the while she had been cool towards him, he had speculated that she might love him. Now that she had declared it, he found himself disbelieving her and imputing low motives to her. He thought that this was all too convenient for Evelyn, that he had appeared just at the moment Julius disappeared; that she had taken up with the first man to offer himself. It had happened to be him. He had been available at the right time. He wondered if any other man would have done to fill the gap. You can either be a romantic and believe that fate has ushered you in at just the right moment, or you can suspect someone of the same sort of pragmatism you have often practised yourself.

'Do you really think that?' he said.

'What?' she said, as though it was all so long ago that she could hardly remember what she had said.

'That you love me?'

'Well, yes,' she said, 'if you want me to be honest about it, I do.'

The way she said it was in self-defence. She wasn't making a declaration any more, only standing by what she had said as a point of honour.

'Would you have loved me in other circumstances?' he said.

It was all dissolved. The atmosphere was gone. He was asking her clinical questions, putting her declarations into hypothesis to see what they were worth. She thought that he couldn't love her. It was an experimental game for him.

'What other circumstances? I have said I love you in these circumstances. Do you think that love is subject to circumstance?'

She said all this coldly, trying to be as cold and interested as he was. She spoke as though they were strangers discussing the economy on a bus. But he had a breast in his hand, and he was studying it. She didn't know if she was capable of maintaining this balance of pretence.

'It's all too easy,' he said. 'You were free. I was free. We liked each other in bed. What if it had been different? What if you were ten years younger and had to give up your children for me? What if you had taken me to bed only to discover that my cock was tiny or crooked or that I liked to do something really peculiar?'

'You don't,' she said. 'It isn't. I wasn't. None of that is relevant.'

She looked at him; gazing at his organ as if its adequacy was a disappointment to him and to science. He was dissatisfied by her answer. He wanted to know if she loved him beyond sex and circumstance. She didn't know whether she did and she didn't care whether she should. She decided that she had made a fool of herself by admitting that she loved him at all. It was an imposition. It was a dent in their affair.

At the moment she said it, she had imagined a gleam of reciprocation. She had thought reciprocation was possible, but she decided now that he didn't love her. That he never could. Why should he? She had him with her for the moment. She had possession of him while he was lame. Shouldn't that be enough for her? What right had she to expect to live at Ryme for ever with a hobbled young lover?

And all at the same time he decided that she didn't love him either. The only reason she could have had for declaring her love was to disguise the absence of love. He wondered why women could never tell the truth. He wondered if it was only that women had a different way of interpreting the truth. He began to touch her again, realising that this time he was lucky to be so level-headed. This time falling in love would be no disaster because he knew already about the deceptions. He knew to keep himself to himself and to keep account of what you have given to measure what you take by.

145

It was plain that she had told him she loved him as a tactic in her lovemaking. She was saying no more than a man would expect in bed. It was a form of flattery that would make him stiffer and more ardent. He thought he would accept her declarations of love, knowing all the while what they really were. He could see that one of the aspects of his own love which proved its depth was his taciturnity. He wasn't coming out with any hollow clichés. But if she had had any real interest in him at all she would have seen the depth of his feeling without him saying a word.

Any temptation he had to be angry with her for not returning his love was lost in the compulsion of their physical contact. He realised that he was lucky to have her at all. He knew that he could soon be dispensable to her. She might get bored with him and anything he could do for her, or he might just run out of excuses for staying within her orbit. He resolved to be grateful for the present and to prepare himself for the smash that was to come.

For now this was enough for each of them. In the early stages of one of these affairs, it is enough to be in the company of the object of your passion. It is only later, when you know someone's weaknesses better, that you will demand a reciprocation.

It was something of an achievement that they got beyond that. Towards the end of February his wounds began to heal but there was no sign of him going to Normandy. He began to make a place for himself at Ryme as though it was his intention that they should always remain there. There was the faintest of hopes that Julius would never reappear, that he might be killed in an accident, or lose his memory. They were prepared to live with this hope until it was disproven.

As he became more familiar with Ryme he also became more assertive in it. He banned Evelyn from the kitchen and they never ate fishcakes again. His culinary repertoire didn't extend much beyond baking salmon and chocolate cake and so, while their food improved in quality, the variety was still limited. He began to bully her in the garden, telling her what she couldn't prune and how she shouldn't prune it. His knowledge was superior to hers, but he had an irritating way of waving his walking stick at the plant in question which, coupled with the arrogant tone of his voice, would make her lose her temper. 'Why do you always have to be right?' she would scream at him.

'Because I am,' he would say in a matter-of-fact, innocent voice that made matters worse.

She felt that Ryme was hers, and he was beginning to feel that it was theirs. When they were half asleep in the evening he would begin to talk about the murder of Julius and their inheritance of Ryme. He had a fantasy about setting the gardens straight and opening them to the public. They would employ Hannah and she could live at the South Cottage. Endless schemes for businesses poured out of him in his half-conscious state. Thirty acres of dried flowers and fish farming. You know all those things that spring into our minds whenever we see a bit of land going to waste.

Much as Evelyn Cotton was in love with Hugh Longford, she could only resent the way he intruded into territory that had been entirely her own. She found attitudes in herself that one would have expected in someone who had been single. She was used to privacy and the comfort of being taken for granted. It began to seem that her marriage had been a loose association of mutual convenience. She was unused to living with someone who demanded a right of access to every part of her life, who constantly demanded to know what she was thinking. She felt herself steamrollered by his enthusiasm. She felt as though choice had been taken away from her, that it was he who decided they should be together, and he who would decide when they were to part.

This was a time that had no reality. The progress of their lives was suspended. Time was occupied in the maintenance of the gardens. They did not work and made no money. More importantly, they made no decisions about the future. They had a vague wish to remain as they were but, in private, each of them was curious to see what would happen next.

I saw Julius at the beginning of March, and he told me that he was about to sell Ryme. He was in a terrible state because Evelyn was proving so difficult. He said that she was forcing him to sell. He collapsed in tears on my sofa. I almost felt sorry for him. But it is impossible to feel sorry for Julius. He was in my house for five and a half hours, and spoke of nothing but his own troubles. Sally had left me the week before, but it never occurred to him to ask how I was, or how the children were. I have never known a man so obsessed with himself; so blind to everyone else.

At about the same time, Hugh got a letter from Normandy,

saying that if he was coming at all he had better come straight away. He asked Evelyn to come to Normandy with him. She could write books while he thatched houses.

She said, 'But you don't want to thatch houses any more.'

He said, 'I know. But I have to do something. If we make a lot of money then I can think about doing something else.'

She said, 'I can't leave Ryme. If I just go now, then Julius can change his mind and move Snagglenickers in.'

He said, 'Let them. Let him. Forget it. What is it to you?'

She disagreed with him by saying nothing.

He said, 'If that is how you feel. If it means that much to you. In that case, the only thing I can do for you is kill Julius.'

She said, 'Oh, be serious.'

He said, 'I will if you will.'

I don't know if Hugh Longford ever really meant to kill Julius. He spoke a lot about it. I think he might have done it if he thought that he could get away with it. Perhaps that is the fine line between a murderer and one of us: a murderer thinks that he might escape the consequences of his crime. Most people, after all, are perfectly willing to kill in the course of a war (what is war if it isn't murder under rules? Genevan genocide?). I know a man who will show you his bare hands, and tell you that he strangled a Japanese soldier with them during the war. Otherwise, he seems perfectly normal and nice. Is the life of a Japanese soldier less valuable than the life of Julius Drake? I know who I would rather share a desert island with. Or perhaps a murderer is someone who is prepared to break a taboo and invite censure. Perhaps murder is an act of courage. It may be better to be a straightforward murderer than to be one of the countless people who fantasise about killing. There is another man I know who leads an outwardly blameless life (apart from weekends with the Territorial Army), but when he is in his cups he has been known to say that as soon as the fascists take over, he wants the job of concentration camp commandant. He also beats his wife quietly. How can you tell that the German nation is morally inferior to any other? How would you be in the same circumstances? Those people are seething beneath the surface of every society. Cromwell was as bad as Hitler. People in America queue up to serve on firing squads. Give me an honest murderer any day: someone with a strong motive or passion. Hugh Longford could only have made the world a happier place by hastening Julius's end.

(Am I being unreasonable? Am I losing hold of my reason, my humanity? In 1968 I would have died for the sanctity of all life. I am a person who will put a bluebottle safely outside a window rather than crush it. Julius thinks that I am his friend. Am I a very peculiar, twisted person? When I read the last three lines of the last paragraph, I am reminded of my father. It was the sort of thing he used to say, with his mouth in an ugly twist. I used to hate him for it. It is surprising how easily you can become a person you used to despise. I now think that I have done Hugh Longford an injustice. Perhaps the whole idea of murdering Julius was a joke to him all the time.)

Hugh talked of murder. If Evelyn had encouraged him, there is no knowing what he wouldn't have done for love. But Evelyn was no Lady Macbeth. She decided to make the whole proposition into a joke, just to be sure. She brought the subject up when they were in company and told everyone what Hugh had said. By broadcasting it as a joke, she felt that she killed off any possibility of him actually doing it. Evelyn wasn't sure how well she knew Hugh Longford.

In any case, they came up to London for a couple of days. That adjusted the perspectives a little. Hugh saw Evelyn at full stretch, among her friends and in her working environment.

Emir Magna and I went to Sarah Bliss for supper the night that Hugh and Evelyn stayed there. That was the first time that I met Hugh. It is an odd thing that I was prepared to like him. I can only say that it must have been because he made her happy. Everyone had said so. Her happiness was a visible thing.

And we all thought that Hugh Longford was a temporary fixture, a tonic for the troops. It was inconceivable that he and Evelyn could last. There was too much of a difference in their ages, in their characters and in their lifestyles. Throughout that supper at Sarah Bliss's, they constantly disagreed with one another. It wasn't bickering, but you could see that they were uneasy with each other. We weren't to know that it was us they were uneasy with. That they only wanted to be alone together, and that it was the presence of other people which spoiled the perfection of their affair. This was something that they didn't know themselves in those days. I looked forward to the day when

Hugh Longford wandered off to continue his own assault on the world, leaving Evelyn to me. I was the man who deserved her most. I had loved her unselfishly for more than twenty years. Who could deny that I deserved her?

Sarah Bliss had, by this time, moved her new man in also. He was a pale, insignificant man and, we all thought, a strange choice for Sarah. His only memorable contribution to that evening was to offer his old flat in Camden to Evelyn. It was a basement with fixed low rent. We all thought it was improbable that Evelyn would ever live there. We had become used to her in the setting of Ryme.

I remember almost nothing of the meal except Emir's explosive laughter. What I remember is the time afterwards, when Sarah's man had gone to bed, and the women were doing some serious drinking around the kitchen table, and I found myself alone in that small sitting-room with Hugh Longford, and he began to talk to me, the way people always do, as though I were nothing more than a confessional box and patently recognisable as such.

But I had decided that I liked Hugh Longford. I thought that I had invented him to bridge the gap between Julius and me. I knew that he would soon exhaust Evelyn. I had slept with a young girl not long before, and had found all that insecurity and virility and curiosity unbearable. The novelty of floundering all over her young body soon gave way to irritation and shame. She made me feel old. I knew that Evelyn must have been feeling old and would soon return to her own kind. Me.

The more Hugh Longford talked to me, the more I liked him. He told me that the most important thing was that Evelyn should write again. When he spoke about her, I could see his desperate love for her. He said that seeing her in London had made him realise how important she was. Until then, he had read her books as one would read private diaries. They had reinforced his idea of her frailty; her goodness and her tragedy. In London he had become aware of her as someone who was an improvement to society. It wasn't that she had transformed herself into another being as she stepped off the train at Paddington. The change was in the people around her. London was full of people who knew how extraordinary she was, and treated her as extraordinary. As he spoke to me, he was in awe of Evelyn Cotton. I think, in his harmless arrogance, he realised that he had found his equal.

Many months later, he told me it was that night, in the single bed of Sarah Bliss's spare room, he decided not to kill Julius. He lay awake for a long time, sweltering in the central heating, with Evelyn packed close to him, snoring with intoxication and pouring with sweat, and in the glare from the streetlights and the noise of the traffic and the East End youths. But he might have slept through all of this if his new perspective on Evelyn hadn't kept him thinking. He decided that to inherit Ryme would be the greatest disaster for Evelyn. Ryme was the thing that kept her battened down, and suppressed whatever it was she was capable of.

He left for Normandy as soon as they got back to Ryme. They were cool in their parting, as if he was only going away for an hour. She climbed the hill after he had gone, to see the daffodils and to see the road he had taken. For no logical reason, she was convinced that he would come back, if only because the affair seemed unfinished.

She immersed herself in Ryme. She wasn't to know that he wrote to her every day, because he never posted the letters. She never really felt that he had left or that she was alone. It wasn't only that she was busy: she had slipped into an easy state of mind. Her life was a perfect balance. She had a lover, and at the same time she was on her own. She had Ryme to look after, and at the same time she was about to begin writing again.

People came and stayed. Now that Julius was gone, she saw her friends from a different angle. She was herself for the first time, and not half of an unlikely partnership. There were perils to being single. Ned Bennet phoned up twice a day to ask if he could do anything for her. Men in general hung about her, waiting to be snapped into the vacuum. Some women pitied her too much. It was hard to explain to them that she was happier than she had ever been. Waiting for your lover to return is much better than being with him. Only anticipated love is perfect. It was hard to explain to people that Hugh was coming back without sounding like a whimsical old maid. So she kept what she felt to herself, and she waited.

Two days before he arrived, all his letters came together. There was a parcel of them. Two hundred and fifty pages. He had written her a novel. She knew that he must love her, and in those last two days she walked about in a corridor of anticipation. They were hot April days and the fritillaries and tulips gleamed in the spring heat and the first rugosa rose leapt at the chance to be free of the winter.

When he found her, she was on the lawn with her wireless playing beside her, and a summer dress spread around her. He walked up to her as if he had only been to the village and back. She smiled at him as if his return was no surprise, but shyly, as though she hardly knew him, all the same. As there wasn't a word that either of them could think of to say, he simply sat down beside her and they fell into lovemaking. Afterwards, he said, 'You didn't come.'

And she answered, 'Yes. But it was nice because I felt you really loved me.'

He restrained his instinct to say, 'I do.' He sat beside her on the warm grass, saying nothing. He felt that it would be inaccurate to say that he loved her. He felt that anything he could say couldn't express what he had felt in Normandy: the overwhelming dark depressing loneliness that had kept him awake at nights, and the daydreams of being with her again that had kept him sane.

She was disappointed that he said nothing. She had waited and saved up things to tell him and, now he was here, it was all an anticlimax, and she felt so deflatingly ordinary when she had thought she should be overwhelmed with passion.

'We are not as happy as we were,' she said.

'I am,' he said. He could give no more away. He felt as if he had come back into the underworld to rescue her. He felt his mission was to get her away from Ryme and away from this lotus-eating life so that she could begin to be herself again. He looked about him at all the gardens and the architecture straining themselves to please him, to seduce him and persuade him that true happiness could only be found with them. He said to her, 'It isn't enough to be happy. You have to be alive as well.' He lay back with his head in her lap and he looked up into her yellow eyes, and he could see that she wouldn't understand, so he said, 'Have you been writing while I've been away?'

'What I wrote in the morning, I shredded in the evening,' she said. 'I knew you were coming back. There was never a doubt in my mind. And it is strange, but the house has never been so benign. It was as if the house was waiting for you as much as I was. When Julius was here you could feel the house bristling. But when I was on my own, it was like being in a trance. I feel the house belongs to us. It is ours by right. I don't know if it would allow anyone else to live here.'

With her hands, she combed his hair back from his forehead. She stroked the soft muscle on his cheekbones. She traced the sharp stubble around his lips. With his head in her lap, he went to sleep.

When he woke, the sun was gone and it was cold. His head was on the grass and Evelyn was nowhere to be seen. Shivering with the cold, he went to look for her. He found her in the bath, with her hair floating on the water behind her.

He said, 'I dreamt that Julius died. Vera Boldt poisoned him, but the police suspected me. They arrested me and questioned me, sitting either side of Julius's corpse. They decided that I was guilty but, just as they were about to take me away, the corpse opened his blue and purple mouth and told them that I hadn't done it. So, I came back here. You were terribly pleased, because Ryme was yours. At first, I was pleased as well, but then I could see that you were a sort of ghost, a servant of the house. I had to save you by destroying the house. You went away for the day, and I set fire to the house, and then I stood outside, watching it burn. I was terribly pleased with myself. All of a sudden, there was a scream from an upstairs window, and you came hurling out of it covered in flames. You had been hiding in the house all the time. You landed at my feet. A broken, charred heap. There was nothing I could do. I opened my veins and lost my blood over your body. As I died I grew colder.'

She was moving rhythmically in the bath, making the water lap about her. She said nothing when he had finished.

'I woke up because it was cold,' he said.

It was all beyond her. She couldn't see what he was sad about or what he was doing with her. Now that he was back, she wondered why he had returned; why he wasn't living in Normandy and falling in love with people his own age. It seemed perverse of him to have chosen her.

'Don't look,' she said, as she made to climb out of the bath.

'Why not?' he asked, looking at her to see what the matter was. She had never suffered from modesty before. Now she was drawing a towel around herself as if he was a stranger.

'Just don't look,' she said. She sounded irritated. 'I am too old.'

He said, 'I don't mind.' He thought perhaps that it was a game, and that he was supposed to be flattering her. Now he felt irritated. He had no time for a coy, romantic affair. He wanted to expose the aspect of her that had been revealed in her books. He wanted her to be incisive, and to observe him and to know what he was feeling every moment and his motive for feeling it. He wanted honesty and rawness. This creature, pulling her towel around her and looking for an easy way to live, she meant nothing to him.

He said, 'Do you really think that you are ugly?'

She said, 'Do you?'

He said, 'Would I be here if I did?'

'You do,' she said. 'You think I am ugly. I know by the way you are looking at me.'

'What way am I looking at you?'

She gave no answer.

He said, 'This is all supposed to be different. Why are you playing the bimbo with me so all of a sudden? There are endless men whose tongues would hang out at the sight of you. If that is all you want, why don't you take Ned Bennet up on one of his offers? What about all those books that you wrote to vindicate the Ugly Woman? And still you seem to want to have builders calling after you in the street. If you were the person who wrote those books, then you wouldn't care how you looked. You wouldn't be fishing for my approval.'

Still she said nothing.

'I am sorry,' he said. 'While I was away, I suppose I built up an idea of you. I lost touch with how you really are.'

'I don't know what you are doing with me,' she said. There were tears in her eyes. He began to take his clothes off. He should have said that he loved her. He knew that he loved her, he had said it to me. But he was withholding it still from Evelyn. Afterwards he said that he hadn't wanted to burden her with commitment.

But now she was crying and he had been the cause. Her crying excited him sexually rather than exciting his pity because if she was crying then there was a touch of reality to the proceedings; she wasn't in that trance; in that corridor of ease and self-possession that she usually held around herself. When he pushed himself inside of her and she was in tears he felt that love had a vitality; that it wasn't just a pleasant feeling and a gnawing at his conscience. Misery was as good as living life to the full.

With his hands, he combed her hair back from her forehead. He stroked the soft muscle beneath her arms. With her head on his shoulder, she finished and went to sleep. When she woke, she was still on the bathroom floor and he had covered her with a duvet.

It wasn't long after all this, after his first return from Normandy, that people began to come and look at Ryme to buy it. It was difficult for Evelyn, but she refused to leave the house until it had been sold. Hugh, seeing that she would inevitably have to leave soon anyway, made no campaign for her immediate removal. Twice a day, the man would come from the agent's to show people around. Life became unreal, suspended between one visitation and the next, like existence in a zoo. The weather stayed warm and the lilacs were early.

Evelyn began to see benign ghosts. She became convinced that the house would allow no one but her to occupy it. They both dreamt constantly of Julius's death. The house was trying to seduce them into staying.

'If you really believe all this,' he said to her, 'then the answer is simple. If the house means you to live here, then you must buy it. Someone else will buy it now, and we will go away, and you will do a lot of writing and, when you have enough money, the house will oust the people who have been here in the mean time and we will move back.'

He said all this in bright sunshine, while they sat among the herbs and stones, drinking their coffee in the morning. He said it lightly, without thinking, or without intending to be taken seriously. But she looked at him as though he had said something credible.

She saw only one flaw in what he had outlined. She believed that he would only stay with her as long as she had Ryme. As long as she had the upper hand and she was the chatelaine. She suspected that he was too strong for her and, once out of her own

155

territory, he would swamp her. She thought they were doomed the moment they left Ryme.

It was that day that an offer was made and accepted. It was as if the house was letting them go, now that they had promised to come back. The new people were dithery, hopeless people. They didn't seem as though they would last. They were only to be caretakers.

Hugh went ahead to Normandy, leaving Evelyn to pack and follow him on when she was ready. It had never actually been decided that she was to go to Normandy, but the idea had settled in, in the absence of another.

She spent a week, wandering through the rooms and tying her books in bundles and putting her clothes in polythene and her china in teachests. She had no idea what the rest of her life consisted of. She was terribly frightened. Horrified by the future, or the lack of future.

When Hugh telephoned her to ask when she would be coming, she said that she wouldn't be coming. That was all she said, and she put the phone down, unable to bear his voice and his questions. He called back and said, 'Look, just don't do anything. I will be there tonight.'

He got back just in time. She had almost gone away. Her luggage had already gone up to London. She had taken the flat that Sarah's new man had offered her. She had taken it in desperation, without seeing it. The address was unpromising, but her instinct for survival was sending her back to London, at any cost.

It was late at night when he returned, and he searched the house for her, calling her name through the bare rooms, afraid that she might be dead or avoiding him. When he found her, she was sitting in a heap in an empty upstairs sitting-room. She was by the long windows that gave out on to the balconies. There was no light in the room save for the light of a weak moon. For want of anything better to say, he asked her what the matter was. She said nothing, and so he sat on the floor beside her.

'It is hopeless,' she said. 'I know that you don't love me. I don't mean it to sound like that. I don't mean that you have an obligation to love me. There is no reason why you should. I always knew that this would be finite. It is a question of knowing when to admit that

156

something is over. It has run its course. I would rather that we parted now, in friendship, than later, in acrimony.' She would have gone on but, when she looked at him, he was swaying in front of her, like a tree that is about to split.

When he spoke, his voice crashed out of him as if he was angry. His declaration came with a violence. He told her that he loved her, and then he repeated it quietly, as though he had to tell himself as well.

Once he had made his declaration, he felt deflated by it. He felt that his position had been weakened. He had nothing in reserve to give her, now that this was given away. It was like all his other experience of women: now that she knew he loved her, he was in her power. The equality between them was lost.

'What are we going to do?' he said.

'I don't know,' she said.

'You are wrong,' he said. 'I am sure that you are wrong. I know that you think I have a compulsion to be right all the time, but this time I know I am right. Perhaps some things have run their course; but I can't see that everything is finished yet. I don't think that this is hopeless or impossible.'

He said nothing more for a while. Probably they did it. There was some sort of hiatus before he told her what he had been thinking all the way from Normandy. London was inevitable.

'You have to move to London, don't you?' he said.

'I can't see what else. I just can't. How could I go and live in Normandy and be supported by you? The vague intention of writing a book isn't enough. I have to do proper work and make proper money. What money is coming in to me now barely covers the interest on my debts.'

'We had better go to London then.' He muttered it.

'Be serious,' she said, 'I can't make you come to London. What would you do all day? You would just wither in London. You once said that you would die in London.'

'I am always saying things,' he said.

'I won't be responsible,' she said.

'You don't have to be,' he said. 'You aren't making me do anything. I have decided. It is nothing to do with you. It is just because I want to be with you. You have to be in London. I don't really have anything better to do, do I? I don't want to be a thatcher the rest of my life. Perhaps this is my great chance.'

'What will you do?' she said.

'Think of a Get Rich Quick scheme,' he said.

'It isn't like that,' she said.

'I know,' he said. 'But I will think of something.'

THOSE LAST TWO days they spent at Ryme were like a vision of paradise before the black reality of death. It was lilac time; it was still that time when all the best things cross over. Where the four orchards met, there was a complete circle of pleached crab apples in blossom, twenty yards across. Within the circle was a thick crowd of lily of the valley, shaded by small apple trees, and still in flower. The scent within the circle was overwhelming.

The stone pavings about the house were smothered in violets and erupted in patches of orange poppies. The hostas were at their plumpest and the ferns were unfurling into tall columns of green between the crushing hordes of Solomon's seal. *Rosa hugonis* was in full flush and, over everything, in every direction, were the lilacs, planted in such a way that you never knew where they were until they were suddenly in flower.

Everything was so extraordinary that it was impossible for them not to regret Ryme as they left it, all new leaves and chestnut blossom. It was the worst time of year for such a wrench, and it was the best, because you thought it could never be better and you had been there at the peak of its beauty while there was still an air of promise about the place.

It rained the day they left. Hugh said, 'Happy is the corpse that it rains on.' Evelyn had no idea what he meant but she was too upset to ask him.

Do you remember that summer? After the end of May, there was no summer at all. It rained from June until the next spring.

Hugh just assumed that that was the way the weather was in London. He had never seen it any other way.

They moved into a basement flat in Royal College Street in Camden. The flat was a horrible place, as all basements must be, but neither of them would say so. They were like a newly married couple making the most of their first place. I went down to them that day, with some food and to see if I could be a help to them. The air was heavy with forced optimism. Everyone was talking about the advantages of living so near to everything; congratulating themselves on living in such an enormous flat for so little rent. And, of course, it was only temporary; a short interlude before they could go up the hill to Hampstead.

Because they believed their own propaganda, that flat may not have seemed so bad to them at first. I wouldn't have chosen to live there. It was a vast cave of a place, with one window in the front and another at the back, and a string of unlit poky rooms in between. Not that much light came in through the windows either. The place had a slight but discomforting smell of damp and drains.

But you had to admire the way they fought it at first. Hugh repainted the whole place, and they went to the opera twice in the first week. They were out to supper every night. They tried their best to exploit every advantage that London could offer. Hugh behaved like a tourist. He went to the British Museum and all the parks and churches. He bought more season tickets in that first week than I knew existed. He tried his best.

From the first morning, Evelyn got out of bed at half-past five and began to write. Every idea that she had had at Ryme and not written down came back to her, in logical sequence. The time she had spent away from London hadn't been wasted. Everything had been stored and filed, and came back out of her faster and better considered for lying in abeyance. Within a month of their arrival she had written the bulk of a large novel.

Hugh had no idea what he would do for a living. He soon got over the pleasure of not being a thatcher any more and of being free to choose what he would do for the rest of his life. His lack of specific ambition began to alarm him. More alarming still was the rate at which he was running through his money. There are few things easier than spending a fortune in London, and what Hugh

Longford had could hardly be considered a fortune. When they met new people, and he was asked what he did, he still had to say that he was a thatcher. There was no other answer to give.

Evelyn was keen that he should get an education. She thought that he should take A levels and go to a London university. At first he was offended by this suggestion. He thought that she was accusing him of intellectual inadequacy, that she was embarrassed by his conversation with her smart friends. This wasn't what she had meant at all, but she stopped suggesting it after a while. By the time he had come around to the idea it was too late. Things had all gone beyond that.

Evelyn became busy. There was hardly a moment in the day when she wasn't working or meeting somebody. Hugh began to be at a loose end. I can't say exactly when this happened. I noticed once when I saw him that he had a sort of tamed look. He was in suspension, like someone in a waiting room. London had defeated him.

It was inevitable that the day would come when he would set out for yet another expedition to Kew Gardens, or a morning hanging around my office, and he would get as far as that pub opposite the tube in Camden Town, and he would see no point in going any further.

If you think that London is an ugly place, there is nothing like drink for making it seem worse. He said that when he was drunk he could see every speck of the plan of filth. He would return to the flat and stand at the top of the basement steps, hesitating because he found it hard to believe that this was where he lived. If he went down the steps he would be lost for ever but, on the other hand, London was behind him, like Scylla snapping her heads. A panic rose in him, and the knowledge that he could get in his car and escape that moment. He need never see London again if he didn't want to. But then he always had to go down into the flat, for Evelyn's sake. How could he leave her without a note, or something? And once he was in the flat he was trapped. When he had shut the flat door and was alone in that long dark hole, nothing seemed possible any more.

He talked to me of plans to find a way of living. He could find somewhere in Somerset to live, and begin thatching again until he thought of something else to do. He and Evelyn could have the

161

weekends together. He only saw her now at the weekends, in any case. There was one time when he almost left and, thinking that it might be the last hour he would spend in it, he allowed himself to see the full horror of that flat. The sordid dank gloom of it. He tried to telephone Evelyn to tell her what he was doing, and he stood with the receiver pressed to his ear and soaked in the repulsive subterranean atmosphere. He watched the legs of people passing in the street and the superior way in which they would glance down through the window at him, superior in the fact that they lived over the ground and he lived beneath it.

The worse the flat and his situation seemed to him, the more pleased he was to be going away. He had never mentioned his intention to leave to Evelyn before. He thought that she might not understand that he was leaving London and not her. She could come with him if she wanted to. But he couldn't reach her on the telephone, and he couldn't leave without telling her first. He had a drink before he dialled again.

She arrived back at eight that night. She couldn't get through to tell him that she would be late because he seemed to have left the phone off the hook. She found him drunk and asleep in the bath. He might have drowned.

She couldn't get any sense out of him that evening. He only wanted to sleep. But in the morning she sat at the side of his bed, and said to him, 'This isn't good enough.'

It was after ten. She had already been up for five hours and had written a newspaper article and cleaned the flat. She was on her way to the BBC for a radio phone-in. She had brought him tea three times, at his own request, and taken it away untouched each time. 'What isn't good enough?' he said.

She said that she was going to open the curtains.

He said, 'No, don't. Leave them. I'll be fine. It's only my head.'

'What is the matter?' she said.

He looked at her through the gloom and knew that he would do no good by trying to explain anything. He knew that she didn't have the time to absorb whatever he would say into her mind.

He tried to make a joke of it. 'You wouldn't understand,' he said, 'I come from a nihilistic generation.'

She made an expression of disgust and impatience. He heard the clatter of her shoes as she left the room and the flat. There was the faint sound from the radio in the next room of a man prophesying her arrival in the studio.

He spent that morning in the gloom, in the dark of his bed, in the faint earthy scents of himself and the cats. He wondered if he smelled different for being a burrow dweller. It was his intention to spend his time in bed thinking about his life and his future, but there was an ache in his head that acted like a barrier of lead sheeting, and no cogent thought could pass through it. In the background, in the other room, there was the voice of Evelyn Cotton, beguiling and guiding the women of the world. He could only catch one word in three, but the sound of her voice was so gentle and suggestive that it was almost sinister. He thought she sounded as though she had no interest in liberating women; as though she was taking pleasure in change for change's sake: a cat who knocks a pencil to the floor, only because she will see it fall.

When he heard her voice on the radio, something in his mind hardened towards her. He thought for the first time that it would be easy to leave and not tell her. Then everything would be up to her, whether she wanted to follow him or not. Whether he mattered to her. Or perhaps she was sick of him by now, and would be pleased to return and find him gone. He knew that he no longer cut a romantic figure. He wasn't the independent, self-possessed man who had strode into her life and given himself when nothing was expected of him. His only place these days was in her bed, not their bed, all tied and packaged and waiting for her pleasure and her next free moment.

He got out of bed, thinking that he might wash the smell of the flat off his body. He would put on clothes that he hadn't worn yet in London, clothes which still smelled of the air in which they had been dried at Ryme. When he walked out of the flat, he would carry no trace of it on him. He went to the bath with a lightness and an optimism that couldn't be sustained.

The oldest cat placed herself on the edge of the bath while he washed. She stared at him in her contemptuous way. He tried to ignore her. She was Evelyn's favourite and the cat he liked least. With age, she had become dirty in her habits. Her dark orange eyes were her last appealing attribute.

She followed him as he dressed, glaring at him and dribbling saliva down her moth-eaten fur. Her coat was coming away from her at the back, leaving a patch of raw pink skin. She watched him closely, as if she was taking note of everything he did to inform Evelyn afterwards.

He stepped over her to go up and put his bag in the car and then he came back again. There was strong sunlight outside and dim electric light within. He left the front door open so as not to exclude the daylight. The air in the flat was unbreathable to him now: the smell of damp and cat litter and the acrid smell of road tarring drifting in through the open door.

When he looked back towards the door, the old cat was squatting on the doormat to pee. He instinctively yelled at her and made a run at her. As he was doing it, it occurred to him that he had no need to be doing it; that the cat and her habits were no longer part of his life. But, as much as it was the cat's custom to piss where she pleased, it had become his habit to prevent her if he could. Hearing his yell, and seeing him run towards her, she shot out of the open door and up the steps into the street; yowling to draw attention to his misuse of her.

There was no screech of brakes or death scream. Only a flattened grey corpse on the road. Apart from the trickle of blood at the corner of her mouth, she bore a sweet expression across her crowded Persian features. She had always worn a cross face in life. In death, she seemed to be a more attractive creature.

He had no idea what you would do with the corpse of an animal who had died in the city. There was nowhere to bury her, and it was probably against the law if there was. He thought he might bury her when he got to the country, and so he wrapped her in a bit of blanket that she had always slept on and put her in a box which he placed beside his bag in the boot of the car. It began to rain.

Happy is the corpse that it rains on. He couldn't go away now. He would have to wait until Evelyn came back. Perhaps she would come to the country with him for the burial, and they would never come back. Perhaps this death would make her realise what a destructive place London was. Perhaps she would see the metaphor.

He went back into the dark flat to wait for Evelyn, leaving the boxed cat in the car. The gloom of the flat began to slide over him. Numbness ran through him.

He tried to think how Evelyn might react when she returned,

but he found that he couldn't even imagine what she looked like any more. The other cats sat around him in a half-circle on the table, all of them watching him with her eyes. They were silent and still, making no attempt at contact with him or each other.

He wasn't very drunk when Evelyn got back. He had been drunker in his time. But she gave him a cross, uncompromising look, all the same.

'This isn't good enough,' she said. She was all set for confrontation. She wanted to fight with him. He could feel her need for a fight, but he had something with which to stop her.

'Muriel is dead,' he said.

It was at that moment; it was that look that crossed her face, that grief and disbelief, that made him realise he still loved her. He loved her more than he ever had. He couldn't go, or leave her, or do anything to alienate her. As bad as his life was here, he could never have any sort of life without her.

I relate the details of all this clichéd love and, the more I speak of it, the less I think it is likely that love exists at all. Love is a convenient blanket term which we use to disguise the complicated reasons we have for wanting to lean on another person. If Evelyn Cotton had married me in 1963, would I have been any happier than I am today? This is not a rhetorical question. It is the question that I should have asked at the beginning. But it has taken me this amount of prose to find the question. I don't feel that I can bore you by making you wait for the answer. If you know the question, that is such an achievement in itself that the answer seems irrelevant. Perhaps the answer is a myth; a decoy to tease us into asking the question. The question is an end in itself. This all sounds like third-rate philosophy. I am sure that someone has said it all before. But nothing seems true until we discover it for ourselves. In a way, Thomas was the only disciple who could think for himself. The rest were so gullible. Pushovers for conversion. Thomas was a man you could hold a rational conversation with.

Evelyn wept for Muriel, naturally. Hugh comforted her. They went nowhere that night. They stayed in Royal College Street, below ground, mourning a grey cat.

Hugh now thought that nothing was as important as being with Evelyn. He thought that he had been petty to want to leave. He kissed her salted kisses on her tears and said that he loved her.

They carried on from this. Although he still wanted to leave London eventually, he made no desperate lunges to escape. When Evelyn began to have a bit of money again, and suggested looking for somewhere better to live, he found himself in opposition to her. He knew that, if they found a pleasant place in London, she would never move back to the country again. His only chance of getting away was if they remained in the basement, and if Evelyn was uncomfortable. Once she was comfortable, it would take Julius Drake to move her.

His money was almost gone. She said that money was not a problem, but he disagreed. He had always had money of his own. Since he was sixteen he had asked no one for money.

It was said that he drank too much at this time. It depends on your terms of reference. He had always been a drinker. Some people are. As all the other aspects of his behaviour receded, and his character began to fade away, his drinking began to stand out from the erosion. I don't believe that drinking was his problem. It was a symptom of his problem. If things had gone on as they were, he might have one day had a problem with drink. But circumstances are rarely static. There came a moment when it looked as though he might make a success of living in this city. The tide came in before it went out further.

He discovered property development. Evelyn had gained enough credibility with Mr Blomfield at the bank to be his backer. He had chanced on an unconverted house in Camden Square. The owner was an elderly Irishman who would sell it to him easily out of compatriotism. Hugh Longford still had enough charm left to be a businessman.

This was perhaps the best of their times in London. It was a time of optimism and anticipation. Evelyn was too busy to think, and she was in love. She had everything she could want, except a decent place to live and, as it seemed to her that they should keep one of the flats in Camden Square, that was no longer a worry to her. She regretted Ryme. She dreamt about Ryme every time that she dreamt at all. They still spoke as though they meant to buy Ryme back one day. In Hugh's new, infectiously optimistic mood, nothing seemed impossible. For a while, the word impossible was intolerable to them.

Things steamed ahead. It was a good time to be an established name in literature. Publishing houses were falling over themselves trying to steal the big names away from each other. Fast as she could work, she couldn't churn out scripts fast enough for the television companies. Hugh found that he could convert Camden Square almost single-handed. Benedict finished at university and, for the want of anything more interesting to do, he came to work for Hugh for a while. They were friends again. It was almost a happy ending for them all.

I remember at that time almost giving up my secret claim on Evelyn. There seemed to be so much natural justice in what was happening to everyone that I wondered if I wasn't mistaken about the whole basis of my life. It began to seem as though everyone got what they deserved in the end. It seemed obvious that I deserved nothing. Have you ever felt that life was a game of Pin the Tail on the Donkey, and that everyone except you had a cunning peephole in their blindfold? I tried to give up my claim on Evelyn and to think about my own life and work out what I really wanted. But I found that I didn't want anything and, frightened by the vacuum beyond my obsession, I returned easily to my obsession, and to my old reasons for bothering to live from one day to the next.

I remember being in a large group of people sometime around then. It must have been a party. Hugh and Benedict were there, but Evelyn wasn't. They asked me to play a game called Spoons. The atmosphere was all hilarity, otherwise my memory of it is dim. I find it hard to recall scenes in which I have partaken, but this memory is sharp and bitter enough in some ways. The game was explained to me. My opponent and I had to kneel facing each other, each of us with the handle of a soup spoon between our teeth. Each protagonist had to take it in turns to hit the other over the head with his spoon.

Hugh Longford knelt before me with his hands behind his back. He almost couldn't keep the spoon in his mouth because he was laughing so much. Benedict stood behind me, keeping score, he said. Hugh's spoon came crashing down on my head. It was more painful than I had expected, but the whole thing seemed to be causing so much sport that I felt I couldn't spoil it by standing up. I tried to hit Hugh as hard as I could with my spoon. It bounced ineffectually in his hair. He grimaced and rubbed his head, as though it had hurt him. I thought the game might be unfair because Hugh had so much hair to cushion the blow, and I only had my bare yellow skull. I thought that might be the joke; the reason why everyone was laughing so much. By the fourth exchange of blows, people were rolling about on the floor with their legs in the air, tears of laughter spurting from their eyes. Hugh was laughing too much to continue. My head was ringing with the blows it had received, but still I was looking around at all the people with a stupid smile on my face.

They showed me afterwards how Benedict had been standing behind me with a third spoon, which he had brought down on my skull with a crack each time Hugh pretended to take his turn. I laughed with them. I took it all in good part and, only afterwards, when I was alone, did I allow myself to burn with shame and rage.

Perhaps you have had enough of metaphors.

I REMEMBER, JUST after Muriel was run over in Royal College Street, Hugh Longford said to me, 'It brings you back in touch with things, death.'

We were sitting in a gloom somewhere. I think it was outside one of those pubs by the river in Hammersmith. I couldn't make his face out. There was a wet flicker where his mouth should have been as he spoke. The London around us, for once, was a silent place. We were waiting for Evelyn.

His voice came in a soft pure tone without a trace of accent. I would have thought that it was someone else speaking, but there was no one else around us. I can't remember the rest of our conversation, or whether Evelyn turned up, or where we went if she did. There is only that sentence spoken in the dark, and spoken as if I wasn't there either.

And I remember the last conversation I had alone with Hugh Longford, and death was the subject again; I felt so close to him that he and I were almost the one person. Our conversation seemed like an internal conversation, taking place in the head of one person. I can't remember any physical characteristic of our voices, as though we spoke telepathically, and had no voices at all.

He said, 'The day that my grandfather was buried was a scorching hot summer's day. My father wore his father's greatcoat to the funeral; out of respect, I don't know, out of admiration, out of reverence; as a penance of sorts. He was white with the heat of the day. I think that my father would like it if I had the same reverence for him.'

'And will you do the same for him?'

'How do I know what I will do? If my father died tomorrow; no, I don't think that I would. But how can I tell who I will be, or who my father will be in twenty years from now? How can I know that it won't be me who dies first? That it won't be him wearing my long coat at my funeral? You can't legislate for anything except the present.'

He spent a long time with me that day. I remember all of it, as if I had recorded it and studied the recordings. I remember it as well as if I had invented it. He used the word goodbye as he left me. Usually, he would have said see you, or something as flippant. I can remember his dished face and mournful chin as he made a last turn before going out of sight.

I saw him once more. Ned Bennet had an exhibition in a gallery in the Finchley Road. We were all there. In retrospect it was like the gathering of suspects at the end of a whodunnit: Benedict, Hugh, Evelyn, Julius, Vera, Sarah, Emir and David, Paul Boldt, Sally, the Bennets and me.

It is hard to know the winter from the summer when you leaf through your memories of things which have happened in London. Sometimes, if you are fortunate, there will be a ceanothus in flower in the background of your memory, and that will place your event within a season. I think it must have been the wintertime when we went to that exhibition of Ned's. It was already dark as I walked down to the Finchley Road. It was raining, but not as cold as it might have been. Perhaps it was the month of March. It seems a long long time ago.

I will tell you. It was three days ago. It was about this time in the evening. There was rain and dark and heavy traffic. I stopped on the other side of the road, looking at the gallery as I waited to cross. I had a bizarre feeling because I could see all of the people who had had a part in my life through the plate-glass window. They came and went, warm and dry but mostly avoiding each other. The only person missing was Simmy. And what was more bizarre was that I had seen Simmy just before I left my house in Frognal. I saw Simmy, and then I walked past the house where Evelyn had lived, and then I came down to the Finchley Road and saw my life in a shop window.

I went into the gallery. The first person I met was Evelyn.

'Guess what?' I said to her. 'I have just seen Simmy.'

'Where?' she said, discomforted rather than amused.

I told her I had seen Simmy on the television. He was playing the farmer who pops the pod in a frozen pea advertisement.

Evelyn said, 'Oh dear.' Her eyes were all pity. This happened from time to time since Simmy had become actor. He had a small part in *Doctor Who* once, covered from head to toe in green slime.

'Don't tell Benedict, will you?' Evelyn said.

'I was just thinking,' I said. 'He seems to be the only one missing tonight. Everyone else is here.'

It was as I said this that Charles Felix came in the door. He looked decrepit and leather-jacketed – more like an ageing pop star than a middle-aged painter. He had a young, thin, leggy girl with him.

Julius Drake wandered the room looking as though no one would talk to him. He was a shivering streel of self-pity. We had heard that Vera had left him, and that he had run through what remained of his friends, boring them with his sorrows, one by one. Now Vera was working her way through the party by herself, rolling her eyes madly at anyone who knew her slightly, or at anyone she thought should know her at all. Paul Boldt was talking to a very short woman. The mulish expression on his face was worse than usual. He was trying to take no notice of Vera, but everyone knew that there was bound to be a scene between them at some point. It was probably for the spectacle of this scene that Ned had invited them both: Evelyn and Julius and Vera and Paul – all avoiding each other. Whenever one of them moved, there was a sort of chain reaction, as everyone tried to keep the greatest distance from everyone else. There were not enough opposite corners in that room to accommodate them all.

Evelyn told me that she had met Julius on the stairs to the basement. She said that she had been cold towards him. It was something she couldn't help. He had looked at her, and burst into tears like a girl. I almost bleed for Julius, now that he is nothing.

Benedict and Hugh were talking. I went over to them. Hugh was saying that he had had enough of the party. He said he would go as soon as he could persuade Evelyn to leave with him. He went over to her, but Evelyn was with Sarah Bliss, talking to Sally. Hugh came back and said he was just off to the pub to wait for her, and would we come too? I said no, I hadn't even said hello to Ned and Hilda yet. I might follow him on. Benedict looked across the room at Julius and said that he should stay here. Someone should talk to Julius.

Hugh Longford raised his eyebrows to heaven and said it was our loss, and he set off across that minefield of a room. He almost moved at a trot in his eagerness to be away. Benedict smiled after him before bracing himself to be nice to Julius. That smile of Benedict's has stuck in my mind. It was the last, frozen moment before the apocalypse.

Across that moment and Benedict's smile, I could hear Evelyn's voice near my elbow. She was talking to the short woman. I could hear her say, 'No tortoiseshell. All my cats are grey.'

It seemed that something was going on in the street. People near the window were aware of it, but because of the rain no one went outside to see what had happened. It was Sarah Bliss's man who came in and stood in the doorway and demanded in a voice louder than his own if any of us was a doctor. It was this man who became the hero of the hour. It was he who, when I went outside, was kneeling by Hugh Longford's head giving him resuscitation. I stood nearby and lamely helped to guide the snarled traffic around us. Other people had taken off their coats to cover Hugh and put behind his head. By the time I realised, it was too late to offer mine. Benedict was swearing because the ambulance was taking so long to come. The driver who had hit Hugh was standing against the wall, sobbing loudly. He was an Italian. I remember thinking he looked too Italian to be real; slightly overweight with tartan trousers and a Benetton green jersey. Somebody was doing their best to comfort him. It can't have been his fault. He couldn't have seen Hugh at all. I had often nearly run people over in the same place, in the dark and the rain. I wrote to the council about it once.

I did my best to keep the traffic moving. The noise of impatient horns came from down the hill, sounded by people who were too far away to know why we were blocking the traffic. There was nothing I could do for Hugh. Other people, more capable than I, were doing all of that. Someone asked if he would live. Someone else said that they didn't know. I said that he was a Catholic and perhaps there should be a priest. I felt unwieldy, once I had said it. It seemed I could be of no practical help at all.

His shoe lay in the road, between the wheels of the traffic coming down the hill. His stockinged foot showed below the blanket of coats. His stocking was a buff colour. I remember at the time thinking that it was the colour of a cardigan which my mother began knitting me when I was four and never finished. It is odd. The texture and colour and shape of his stockinged foot is my clearest memory of that night.

Evelyn was saved from hysterics by the example of Julius's uncalled-for histrionics. He was determined to be a Mary Musgrove, to the irritation of everyone. He was sent away with five sharp words from Evelyn, and he went back into the gallery.

An ambulance got through the traffic in the end and took Hugh and Evelyn away to the Royal Free. I went back inside for a moment. Ned Bennet was pacing up and down. He hadn't come outside at all. He was repeating to everyone in turn, 'It wasn't our fault. What could we do? It could have happened to him anywhere. It wasn't our fault.'

I went home on my own. Because it was in my interest for Hugh Longford to die, I couldn't afford to allow myself to think that night. If Hugh Longford died I didn't want the guilt of wishing him dead. Hugh had become a friend of mine and I had a fondness for him outside of my love for Evelyn. I took a couple of sleeping pills and went to bed.

PERHAPS I OWE you an apology. Perhaps I have alarmed you unnecessarily. Hugh Longford is not dead. He is in no danger. His complete recovery will be a matter of months perhaps: he has broken some bones and bruised some organs; he has lost a bit of blood. There is nothing wrong with him that cannot be fixed.

It is odd that I should apologise to you. I have no idea who you are; whether you have come to care about Hugh Longford, or whether you are someone who knows him in real life, and loves him there. I have addressed you for all these pages and your face is a blank to me. Perhaps you are nothing more than my own compulsion to set this down. I sat down this morning with an itch in my fingers; with a need to exorcise certain things by putting them on paper. I could not write into a void, and so I called you into being, and what contact have I with you? Run your hand along the back of your neck, as at this moment I am running mine: and now we are both feeling the same thing at the same moment, we have had a sort of consummation, you and I. Still I have no idea who you are.

But I began to write this and so I must finish it. I feel I have been writing this for a year, but still I think that it was only this morning I started. I can't know for sure. This has been like a hibernation; a sleep. It might be this morning; it might be last month. I think it must have been this morning, because I can't remember eating since I began, and I am no thinner.

I began this because of yesterday. Because yesterday I had

everything from ecstasy to humiliation. Evelyn Cotton came back to me, and I was punished by the granting of my wish.

For a day I had felt nothing but relief. I was grateful to God for the life of Hugh Longford. I had been prepared to profit by his death. When he was lying in the Finchley Road, at the back of my mind I was thinking If he dies now; if he is dead – then Evelyn. If he had been killed by natural justice, and Evelyn had been given to me, I would have stepped up to take her. And then the guilt, the burden of wishing a man dead to take his wife; and, even more than that, Uriah Longford was my friend. Just as I had no courage to wish him dead in the front of my mind, so I couldn't have been brave enough for the guilt of profiting by his death.

So, yesterday, Evelyn Cotton came to talk to me, in the middle of this relief of mine. If I was expecting her, it was only that she has come to talk to me in every crisis. We are friends in a way we could never have been friends had we ever married. There are times when I feel that her confidence in me is a great compliment. Other times I know that she only confides in me because I am harmless. I am not going to make a fiction of a confidence and broadcast it, as Ned Bennet would. I haven't got the courage to betray, or to enjoy myself at her expense. I am not clever enough to be a false friend. I am her friend because of my impotence and not because of any power over her. I am a perfect friend because I barely exist.

It seemed obvious to conclude that Evelyn was in shock. When she came into my house she looked terrible. Her skin was grey and her eyes were red with weeping. We talked for a while about our relief over Hugh, and then she said, 'I am leaving him.'

'Hugh?' I said.

'When he gets out of hospital he will have to lead his own life. None of this is good enough. If it has to end, it may as well be now.'

I said nothing. I had nothing to say. I must have sat for a long time gaping at her with nothing at all going through my mind.

Then she asked me if I had a drink in the house. To my embarrassment I realised that I only had champagne. For years I had kept a secret store of champagne against the day when she would come to me. I had hidden it as a schoolboy hides a condom in his pencil case; in hope rather than expectation.

Evelyn broke from her coldness and laughed out loud when she saw the champagne. Perhaps she thought that I was making a grotesque joke. And there was sort of madness in her laughter. She was not herself. She was like one who is bereaved; who is unstable because of loss. And I thought of the Chinese girl in Clifton. She laughed because laughter was the only emotion she could express without losing face.

I thought of something to say, at last. I said, 'But I thought that the two of you were happy?'

'We were,' she said.

I pushed the cork out. It was hard not to think of the sexual metaphors in opening champagne. I turned away from her, as though opening the bottle was a private thing. Not a thing you did in front of a lady. I could almost hear my mother making a prohibition on the subject.

I set one glass down and filled it for her. She asked me why I wasn't having any. I said, 'It gives me asthma. I thought you knew that.'

I was slighted by this, by the proof that she had no interest in the minutiae of my life. I knew every like and dislike of hers. I knew the birthdays of all her relations. I could remember which brand of athlete's foot solution she used. This way in which she could slight me without her being aware of it was something I have borne for twenty-five years. I should be used to it by now. I will never be used to it.

As she drank the champagne, bottle after bottle, so she began to talk to me. She was wrong to have taken over Hugh's life. She was wrong to have allowed him to fall in love with her. It was selfish to waste his youth. Since they had moved to London, her guilt had doubled. She had made a ghost of him. She had tied him down in a place where it was unnatural for him to live. She had watched him fade away.

I said, 'Perhaps he would have faded away, anyway. Perhaps he needed to grow old, and perhaps he chose you because he wanted to fade away.'

I could never express things. I could see that Evelyn had no idea of what I meant. She looked at first as though she might take offence, and then she just relaxed into incomprehension. She shook my diffuse remarks off her, and went on talking as though I had said nothing.

She said that she had watched Julius fade away in Somerset. But that was no trial to her. She had never loved Julius. His fading away had made her life easier. Her destruction of Hugh Longford was an agony to her.

She didn't think, she said, that it was possible for two people to flourish if they lived together. One person must feed off the other. One person will be strong and the other person must be in decline. In the beginning Julius had dominated and fed off her, but it was through Julius's transparency that she had observed and learnt how to be the survivor. He had taught her selfishness by example. That is all her books were, did I know, an exhortation to women to be selfish.

And she had been selfish and lived at Hugh's expense, and he had faded and become almost nothing; become so insignificant that a hired car could almost end his life.

But she had always known that she and Hugh had a finite amount of time, that Hugh must want a proper wife and some children of his own one day. It couldn't be healthy to have children who were of your own generation. And she knew that the longer they stayed together, the more difficult it would be to separate. At first she had thought that in time they would drift away from each other but, as it was, time made them more and more dependent on each other, and so, did I see, it had all become hopeless.

And then she said she and London, between them, in collusion, had caused the accident; had almost killed him. It was a warning.

Now she was doing the good thing and the brave thing. She was being a self-sacrificial heroine, forsaking all for his sake and stuff. She had left him because she loved him.

All the time she was looking at me in a way I hadn't seen for more than twenty-three years. I was too slow; perhaps too concerned for her (if, for once, I am generous to myself), to realise what she meant by that look, and what she had meant by coming here at all.

Perhaps she never meant any of it. Perhaps it just happened this way. Or I took advantage of our friendship and the fact that she had drunk too much.

And it wasn't anybody's fault; this thing which I had craved for most of my life. I said that I had better turn the light on, and when I had turned it on I looked at her and tears were coursing down her face.

'I am sorry,' I said.

I am not a physical person and I get embarrassed when people cry, and my children have all accused me of being an inadequate father because I never showed them physical affection but, somehow, this time, this once, it was easy, and I went and put my arms around Evelyn Cotton to comfort her.

I had no intention of anything but comfort, but can you expect a hungry man to give comfort to bread? When we were kissing, it was like hungry children who have never kissed before.

She stood up and she led me upstairs by the hand as though it were her house and not mine, and as though it was she who needed me. And at the back of my mind I thought This is what she came here for all along. She came here to seduce me; to cement her sundering from Hugh. She came here because she was sure that I would want her; that I would be prepared to betray Hugh Longford. And here I am, following her up my stairs, unable to control what is happening in my own trousers.

And she unbuttoned my clothes as though they were her clothes, not mine. She touched me as though she was touching herself.

This sounds like a penny dreadful romance to me now. It embarrasses me to admit that for a while I went through a euphoric happiness, and I lost any consciousness of my self, of my unwieldy, ugly body, of my feeble mind.

Why I couldn't have been grateful for this happiness; for this perfect ending? Why I couldn't have continued with that weight-less soaring over Evelyn Cotton? Hugh had his life and I had her and, as she said, this betrayal was for Hugh's own good in the end.

But the sound of her voice brought me crashing to earth. Her voice was artificial; trying too hard to be erotic. She was speaking to me as a whore will speak to her client. She could sense the approach of my climax and she was faking her own to coincide with it. She can't have known that I knew her so well. That I retained an imprint in my brain of the sound of her voice in pleasure. This was the sound of her voice in condescension, in charity. This voice cut through my euphoria, and made me an old man again; floundering and wriggling over her like an oversized tadpole; kicking my thin legs and spinning on my stomach.

Ashamed of myself, I climbed off her before I should have, and asked her why we were doing it.

'For you,' she said.

And then she said, 'No, that is wrong. That is patronising of me. I wanted to sleep with you because of my love for you.'

I was quivering. I had lost control of myself. My teeth were chattering. My stomach was shaking as though it would explode. An unfinished erection clung below it, waving helplessly. There was no part of me with any dignity left in it.

She had said what I wanted to hear and, at the same time, I was shivering with excitement – and with rage because it was a lie. But rage in me is a timid thing. You would need an expert eye to spot it.

'That isn't true,' I said.

'No,' she said.

And then she said, 'But it is as true as anything else. I am fond of you and I like you and you have been a friend to me. I feel guilty for all the the years that you loved me and I have given you nothing, and so I feel indebted to you. I want your companionship and I want your protection. These things, all together, must add up to love. What else could love be?'

'Lust,' I said.

'What, that?' she said. 'This? This in isolation is nothing.'

My genitals shrivelled beneath me as she said it. It was as though she had dismissed them, and they buried themselves beneath the overhang of my stomach.

'No,' I said. 'That wasn't what I meant. By lust I meant compulsion. I meant that if you loved me, you would be obsessed with me, as I am obsessed with you. By lust I mean that there is no choice. You wouldn't be here only because of some game you are playing with Hugh. You are doing this for Hugh; not for me. It isn't my turn yet.'

She was in tears again and I was her comforter. I put my arms about her and we got properly into bed, lying close like an old married couple. Her flesh on mine.

And I thought that I had said my piece, but kept her all the same; I began to think that now that the air was clear we could start again, and I made to move over her, but she was asleep, and I let her sleep.

She slept for hours: me beside her; tormented with wanting her; convincing myself more every moment that when she woke she would want me for myself. When she woke she would want to stay with me.

When she woke, in the middle of the night, I was still ready for her, and my mouth was burnt dry with the hours of waiting in the state I was in. I pressed myself to her but she tensed to me and she said, 'No, it isn't fair. We have gone beyond that. It will only make things worse.'

'But I want to,' I said. 'I don't mind. I don't mind.'

I could feel she was weeping again, and her weeping dissolved me. She said she should go. It wasn't fair. I said no, I would go to another room. She should sleep.

And she was asleep again while I was still talking to her. It seemed that she hadn't been awake at all. I convinced myself that she had spoken in her sleep, and that my promise to sleep in another room wasn't binding.

I put the lamp on; it was a soft light and I sat on the bed, between her and the light, throwing a Buddha-shaped shadow over her. I sat without moving and watched her for the rest of the night.

It is difficult to say when I decided to kill her. It seemed to be the only way to jam an iron bar into the spokes and stop everything just where it was. Life would never be better than this. Why go on with it? There was nothing left to wait for. You only get one or, at the most, two moments of bliss in this life. There was nothing to look forward to but frustration and decline.

I had sat the night, naked and crosslegged on the bed, welded by cramp into position, combing my fingers through the fur of my stomach. I wanted to be awake and watching her for every moment of her that was left to me. I didn't want her to wake up and leave me.

I went to get a knife from the kitchen. Because the circulation had stopped my legs gave way beneath me. I hobbled slowly through the pain and the pins and needles, downstairs, massaging my calves as I went.

Did you ever think I could? I brought the knife and held it against her backbone. I couldn't even make the blade touch her skin. I was afraid that the cold of the blade would irritate her. Her broad, smooth, warm back. I cried because once I had been a thin young man whose body fitted into the contours of her back and backside. Or did I cry because I was mourning the loss of her in advance? Like the queen who screamed first.

There have been moments today when I wished I had killed her. If I had killed her, then some part of her would still be here. I wouldn't be in this void; this vacuum. I might never have filled these endless sheets of paper.

Evelyn Cotton slept on. She slept soundly into the morning. Probably it was the first time she had slept since Hugh was run over. By the morning, I had been watching her for so long that I thought perhaps I possessed her. Or that she possessed me. It didn't matter which. I would have gone into a decline for her. I would have watched myself fade away quite happily to be in her company.

I left her in my bed and went to shower. It is bizarre: we are now talking about this morning; today. It might have been a year ago, but it was only this morning that I stood in the shower watching the water course over me, without a word of this written. I stayed in the shower for a long time, watching my body hair run straight in the flow of the water; reconciling myself to myself; trying to see that Evelyn need not be revolted by me. But she was never revolted. She never felt anything as strong as revulsion for me.

I am not handsome. But I looked in the shaving mirror and thought that my beard must go. I had grown it a long time ago; I had tried to hide behind it. But how can you hide someone who is already invisible? By trying to hide him you cause him to stand out. I looked in the shaving mirror and Captain Haddock stared back out at me, and I knew that the black fuzz had to go from my face.

And for what? Fifteen hours later my jaw is rough again. I remember now why I grew the beard. I grew it because, as I shaved every morning and evening I was reminded of the relentlessness of life. Shaving was the most depressing ritual for me.

When I had removed my beard this morning, I thought that I didn't look too bad beneath it. There were terrible black hairs sprouting from my nose, and so I snipped them with nail scissors. I found that I was amused by my own vanity.

I went out to buy breakfast for her. It was spring in Hampstead. I bought croissants filled with chocolate and almonds, and I bought armloads of lilies and daffodils, and the best coffee and Benedictine to spike it with. I knew what she would like best.

And when I came back she had woken and gone. Everything I brought for her is still there, at the other end of this table. I should have put the flowers in water. They look as though they might be dead by now. I could have brought them round to Hugh. He is keen on flowers. I don't know if anyone else will remember to bring him some. It isn't something you bring to a man. Why?

Why has she gone back to him? Why does she love him and not me? Would it make any difference if she did love me? Wouldn't I just have found something else to complain about all this half-life of mine? Wouldn't I just have become obsessed with something else I couldn't have? I had children of my own, but I preferred to be a father figure to Benedict and Hugh Longford. I have never been able to value anything that was my own. If this is so, is it better that I never possessed her?

And all these questions and all these pages lead to another question which, if you put it simplistically, is: Is this life of mine worth pursuing?

And I can't think of one thing which justifies my existence. I sat down this morning with an itch in my fingers, and now that itch is almost gone. I will have finished writing this before we know the end of the story. This is unfair to you. Why should you be denied an ending?

Let me guess an ending for you. I should be right. I know all of these people better than they know themselves. Let me tell you what the end will be.

She and Hugh Longford will go to Normandy, or somewhere that he can be his own man. Being away from London won't stop her writing this time. They will have as much happiness as is humanly possible. She will never tell him what happened yesterday and neither will I. Because they deserve to, they will survive.

Benedict will have children. Quite soon, I think. Julius will dwindle into nothingness. Vera Boldt will go on ricocheting through other people's lives until she drops down dead.

That is all I need to tell you. Using these principles it is easy for you to work out what will happen to the rest.

And me?

I thought this morning that I was going to kill myself for certain.

182

If I hadn't begun to write this I would be dead by now. There have been times in this narrative when I have changed my mind because while I was writing I had a purpose. Now the writing is finished and I have no purpose. There is nothing I can think of to justify my existence.

Perhaps I will go on living through cowardice. How do I know that I will be able to do this thing? We will see which is stronger: On one side is my self-hatred; my disappointment; my worthlessness; and on the other side is my cowardice. One side will feed off the other.

But then I am living. Since yesterday my emotions have been scraped raw. I have been alive for the first time in a long time. But at whose expense? To go on living like this would be to bring misery to her and to Hugh Longford. I would need to be as selfish as Julius or Vera Boldt. I don't have the nerve to live life the way they do. But I think I might have the nerve to die.

I will remove this stomach from in front of me. It is the part of myself that I hate the most. It will be a pleasure to remove it. I will be a slim corpse. They can bury my gut separately. It is nothing to do with me. As I write I am opening my shirt and the top of my trousers. The last person to undo these buttons was her.

It is here: this round, hard thing covered in hair. I can't believe it will be a problem to take it away.

FRANK RONAN
THE BETTER ANGEL

At seventeen, John G. Moore was in need of salvation. Afraid of the dark and of inheriting his mother's madness, he found irresistible the arrogant assurance of a newcomer to his Irish country school – the eccentric Godfrey Temple. Then John G. began to notice the cracks in Temple's patina. Tracing their volatile, doomed friendship, this powerful narrative captures the wit and anarchy of youth and the often painful transition to maturity.

'As exceptional as its predecessors . . . Ronan is as gifted as anyone from his generation, probably even from the next one up. His prose, understated and fluid, provides consistent and enormous pleasure; his exposures of the human heart are performed with a surgeon's skill and patience'
The Sunday Times

'Excellent . . . something of an Irish LE GRAND MEAULNES'
GQ

'Written in a limpid precise style that's resonant but never overwhelming . . . Ronan paints the understated anguish of his characters with wit . . . extremely readable'
Time Out

'Marked by an eloquent and generally taut style . . . Ronan is excellent in tracing the relationship between the awkward and late-developing John G. Moore and the friend he hero-worships'
The Sunday Tribune

SCEPTRE

FRANK RONAN
A PICNIC IN EDEN

Does the world allow for true love between a man and a woman? And if not, can one call the friendship between two men love? Adam Parnell, an expatriate Irishman, and Dougie Millar, a taciturn Scot, are in different ways looking for a return to innocence, living with their wives amid the beauties of the Western Isles. Both men find in each other the means to confront their childhoods – and the demons that drove one of their fathers to drink, the other to suicide – and to discover whether, once left behind, there can be any return to Eden.

'An extraordinarily fine writer . . . his novel is a shifting tableau of brilliances and oddities . . . The precise lyrical beauty of the prose – poetic but never purple – is a vehicle for a disturbingly dark vision, for gut-punching philosophies and flashes of wit'
Elle

'A rich and assured look at the ways parents can sour a child's capacity for adult love . . . Ronan has an impressive wisdom and breadth of vision'
Cosmopolitan

'An absorbing novel . . . Ronan is a relentlessly honest, quirky and exciting new writer'
The Daily Mail

'Crisp and elegantly written'
The Observer

'Makes one impatient to see what this writer will do next'
Times Literary Supplement

'Ronan writes in an easy, limpid style; he has fluency and a light touch'
Independent on Sunday

'A PICNIC IN EDEN continues in the same rich literary vein he tapped so successfully with THE MEN WHO LOVED EVELYN COTTON'
The Times

'Both refreshing and often disturbing'
The Irish Press

SCEPTRE